ONE BEAUTIFUL
DAY TO COME

ONE BEAUTIFUL
DAY TO COME

A NOVEL

ROBERT LALONDE

TRANSLATED BY NEIL BISHOP

Ekstasis  Editions

Canadian Cataloguing in Publication Data

Lalonde, Robert.
[Belle journée d'avance. English] One beautiful day to come

Translation of: Une belle journée d'avance
ISBN 1-896860-34-6

I. Bishop, Neil B. (Neil Breton)
II. Title. III. Title: Belle journée d'avance. English.
PS8573.A3835B4513 1998   C843'.54   C98-911041-9
PQ3919.2.L19B4513   1998

The original French, *Une belle journée d'avance* was published in Paris France by
Editions du Seuil, 27, rue Jacob, Paris Vle, in 1986.

Published in 1998 by:
Ekstasis Editions Canada Ltd.

Box 8474, Main Postal Outlet   Box 571
Victoria, B.C. v8w 3s1   Banff, Alberta TOL OCO

THE CANADA COUNCIL | LE CONSEIL DES ARTS
FOR THE ARTS | DU CANADA
SINCE 1957 | DEPUIS 1957

The translation of *One Beautiful Day To Come* has been done with the assistance of the
Canada Council for the Arts Translation Program. *One Beautiful Day To Come* has been
published with the assistance of a grant from the Canada Council for the Arts and the
Cultural Services Branch of BritishColumbia.

For my daughter Stéphanie,
in memory of a beautiful storm at the little lake

"When mysteries are very clever, they hide in the light. Shadows are just tricksters."

Jean Giono

"I know this orbit of mine cannot be swept by a carpenter's compass."

Walt Whitman

Contents

I am not yet born. Not even in the egg yet. Not yet that squirming little tadpole. Not yet one of yours. However, it will happen very soon. As folks say hereabouts, "I'm doing Easter before Palm Sunday." I am celebrating right now, spellbound by it, deep within my limbo – life coming. As though I were seeking a world in which to slip my joy, my obsession with beauty one can touch, embrace, my fear of emptiness. I know where I shall arrive, like a flower at the tip of its stem. It is to be, like spring after winter, so has it been decided. But meanwhile, such mystery, such whispering!

Imagine a breath seeking a mouth, a spark running through a field, a ferocious little hope: that's me!

Dawn

You say to me: "Stay, my love." So again I give you my long, gentle weight, I sink onto your breasts, onto your belly drenched with our sweat, and breathe strongly as waves upon your ear. Outside, a heavy summer rain is cleansing up the world, and it was about time: we were suffocating beneath a black sky that, for three days, weighed upon us like a spell. The book was no longer making headway, the pages scowled, the ink was becoming frighteningly pale. Now, through the open window, we can hear the cool sound of the storm and it smells of new grass, peonies, and clean sand. You say to me, "Do you think he's started?" I shrug that I don't know, with my hand on your back, my fingers climbing up and down the hollow between your shoulder blades. I raise myself onto my elbows, I look at you, your eyes are saying "If he is not yet a part of me, he is very near, just there, right at the brink of life, he wants to plunge in, I know it, he'll come."

They dive through the mist. They are still just that vibrating trail swelling and thinning, swelling again from south to north over the big lake. As far as Three-Pine Bay you can see their wavering festivities in the world's sky. They are this singing murmur, this moving galaxy, this beautiful sign of summer. After travelling blindly through so many countries, after so much foreign sky, they are finally entering our sky: the tufted ducks. The one leading the flock, "the raftsman," as Maurice, my father, will teach me, is already piercing the veil of mist above the wharf. There he goes into a breathtaking dive, exhausted, yet so sure in his fearsome plunge! He has recognized the stand of bulrush in front of the large white house, those with that good, slightly bitter taste last summer. Together the others descend, following him. They are like some constellation sliding star by star into the lake. Their wings become intermingled with those of the garish mallows come to smell, to hear news of the far-off South. The cove chatters like a carnival. They're here!

They first got a glimpse of the huge headland, the dragon's tail with its spruce clawing the horizon, its vast, safe bay. Already their flight was slowing down, full of hope. And then they saw the Indians' cove up ahead, the weather-beaten cabins, the rows of tranquil pines already bursting with sunlight. Then, the main street, the only one – it's called "main street" nonetheless, that sounds more serious – bordered with still-dry poplars. Finally, the church steeple, radiant this infant morning. The village. Immobile, the same as it was last autumn and the spring before. At the far end of the village, had they gone to see, the lake continues. We are a peninsula. Nearly an insula. The village almost floats upon the large blue lake. We are isolated, at the end of the world, immobile. You come back a little, three wing beats, and all of a sudden, there is the church, thrice burned down by the Indians, thrice rebuilt. Us folks, we need the good Lord. We need a shrine, three Low Masses, protection. Behind is the mountain. An ordinary mountain, billowing with new leaves. The fiery face of the sun is just now emerging from behind it, immediately dazzling. Across from the large white house, soon to be mine, the ducks rest. They are still quivering, full of Mexico and Virginia.

And there you have it. Things and people are going to start moving, with their faithful shadows, nothing very extraordinary. Only...

But who is that, already up and about?

In a row boat moored to two poles planted in the mud, Jacob and Germain are fishing. They have already caught twelve small perches and one puny walleye. Before, the walleye would have been returned to the water so that it could grow some more. But seeing how long it was since one from mid-depth had last been caught, there was no way they would throw this one back. Wriggling, fine, sparkling proof this evening, on the wharf: what a godsend! People had been wondering where the walleye had gone. To spawn in which waters? Gone to nose around what islands? Seduced by the beautiful channel of what river? I have a good mind to put that puny walleye in tune with my own passion for source and childhood. My passion for this nascent day and its passion for rivers: birth passions. We are too curious, the little walleye and I.

So, there they are, fishing quietly away, Jacob and Germain, the two cousins. After this day now beginning, they will no longer be called otherwise than "the two innocents." And with good reason, that's for sure!

They trot along. Their skirts stiff and their rosaries jingling. The three little nuns from the nuns' convent are off to hear mass. Even purgatory is a hell. Must remember that, at all costs, remember that! They greet Louis the barber who is sweeping his front steps.

"Good morning, Louis."

Which one spoke? Impossible to guess. The voice was muffled in their wind-filled veils. The peace of an endangered soul depends on them. Quick! Quick!

Louis is sweeping. He is getting ready. His barber shop is the town sounding-board. Speak, retract, get it wrong, mix up names and stories and then un-mix them two weeks later when your hair has grown back and is tickling the nape of your neck.

Raising his head to try and glimpse the contours of this brightening world, Louis sees the ducks just as they are finishing their descent from the sky.

"They're here!"

While that is all he says about it, it is not all he thinks. But he is getting ready. He will speak later. When they will listen.

Malvina, my aunt, has finally put her nose out the door. She is seated, arms crossed, on the veranda step. She is shivering. The big white house is empty. Sam left. He had taken up the bottle again, his faithful darling. His own mermaid, his poison. Malvina has just experienced three days and three nights of a calamitous drowsiness. The letter is already in the box, at the end of the little path. For two days, the letter's been waiting. Acrid, pale little morning. Malvina doesn't think about the mailbox. She thinks: "Will I be cured yes or no? Does one get over this?"

A single chestnut tree in the village. People call it "the tar-nut tree". A name like any other except that it sings, like all the names people invent when they live far from dictionaries. Lying under the star-nut tree, the mechanic's dog is licking his paw. He has hurt himself again. Roaming, mongrel, abandoned. About ten moons ago, it was: the mechanic piled all his old stuff into a cart and left. The dog wanted to follow him, but the mechanic hit him and fled, whipping his horse with all his might. The dog ran to the foot of the big hill, but did not go up. He sat there, devastated, crazed. Disappointed. What's the point of following a cart that'll take you nowhere? He licks his chafed paw meticulously, under the chestnut tree. He is always tearing some piece of himself, a paw, an ear, or the tip of his muzzle. Crazy dog, as they will say. For him too the coming day will be full of breathless surprises.

On the highest branch of the star-nut tree, a sparrow is singing at the top of its voice. Is it hungry? Is it happy? How can you tell? But it sure is singing!

And the sun is fully risen.

Curled up in the heart of the world, alive, before life, before cradle and light, before the white house and the lake, before the village, here I am. I will tell you as I go along about the flashes that will quicken me like foretastes. No clairvoyance, no premonitions, not even visions. I am coming. Patience! Even if it is difficult. Life calls, it is forever calling. We must be born. We must come into the world. I shall tell you how beautiful it is to sense, in the blood of namelessness, life growing. I shall tell you as I go along. Patience.

Day has risen in the village. First day of summer. First day of the world. Patience, my love!

Morning

The mechanic's dog is meandering. The morning is still cool. Malvina, who sees him pass by, his nose in the air, his tail wagging, thinks, "I don't like that ugly dog nor any other dog, they're dirty, their big paws..." And she thinks no further about dogs, neither this one nor any other. Her heart ceaselessly, alas, returns to the same bitter pain: "Sam! He has hit the road again, drunk when he came the last time in his over-sized Sunday-best suit to tell me: 'I'm going, Vina, and the devil knows when you'll see me again, my beauty!' For starters: beautiful, no. Not me. That I am not. Simply alive, and kind of wishy-washy, like they say down at the inn, those men who drink with him."

The dog has stopped. He is sniffing the grass, he is searching, searching for he knows not what. His muzzle draws him on, he is excited. The unknown is nettling him this morning. The dew gives a tempting savour to all that gleams in the grass.

"Don't come any closer, you! Or I'll give you a bang with my shoe!" Malvina has taken off her shoe which she brandishes, the heel raised high, quite fearsome. But the dog goes on without even seeing Malvina's armed heel, her menacing spinster's distress.

"Sam!" she cries out despite herself, inside herself, someplace where not the slightest echo repeats the name so dear, so hated with love, and it is sad, sad that name which goes off all alone in the emptiness of her breast where nothing echoes but blood that churns, churns nonetheless, and which is too abundant, too murky, like a river after the ice breaks up.

She sits down, Malvina, in the big, high-backed chair. She takes a deep breath so as to give the blood its food, its quota of air so that it will continue to rush through her, so that it does not suffocate her, so that it will not dam itself up, never become a sea, an ocean to swallow, never never ever!

The dog, meanwhile, has reached the water's edge where the frogs have been waiting on him to play, to put him into his mad dog frenzy.

"These are his kisses. This was his mouth, his taste, his smell of sweat mixed with his slightly spicy cologne. That is the hardest part. His body that used to suddenly collapse upon mine, unleashing its life-force. Sam!..."

Malvina runs her large white hand over the rough wood of the chair. "That is what is hardest: his body, gentle and strong and now gone." And so she gets up, and, somehow or other, heads down the path towards the mailbox.

Jacob plunges the oar, and at once his elbow vibrates with that wrong vibration.

"I'm touching the bottom. We're going to run aground!"

Germain says, "Of course not! It gets deeper right after."

And Jacob, right away indeed, almost loses the oar from his hand as it plunges deep. And Germain smiles.

"I know this lake like the back of my hand!"

And Jacob says, "Yes."

And nothing else. Then he waits. He waits for the sign Germain will make with his head when he knows where to drop anchor. The water lilies, when the boat passes over them, murmur in protest. A shivering sound, like soft flesh being crumpled, so that you have the very unpleasant feeling of doing wrong without being able to do otherwise. "Disturbing nature sure doesn't bother some people," thinks Jacob. "Some people even fish with dynamite, at night, and with motors leaking their oil as though it was natural. But it makes me sick, it bothers me to bother the lake. And I don't say anything. If I did, I'd seem dumb. Sissy picky. But it hurts me to crush the beautiful water lilies, to disrupt nature, to live my life by pushing around beings and things that were here long before me and have earned their place, because..."

"The anchor!"

Jacob had forgotten to watch for the signal. Of course.

"On the moon! Jacob, you're always on the moon!"
"Are there water lilies on the moon?"

In Louis the barber's doorway. The glass column they call the "thick stick," with its red spiral that rises, turns and disappears without ever disappearing, fascinates Alcide who puffs on his pipe, one hand on his very round, plump, ever so soft paunch.

"Where's it come from and just what's it for, Louis, that there thingamajigger?"

And Louis, in his blue barber's coat, his discreet smile beneath his discreet mustache, answers,

"Well, to tell you the truth, Alcide!..."

In other words, there are sometimes in the world, and particularly in this village, things like this, things come from somewhere else and that have no explanation, that make people shrug their shoulders in a gesture of quiet ignorance. Things from the old country or from the giant to the south, and which are there because. Imported mysteries, whose meanings and origins have remained captive, clear only in the memories of a few ancestors who did not deign to teach, who perhaps did not even know themselves. Because, sometimes, that's the way things are! Secret, impenetrable, and so they become the stuff of idle talk. Like Louis the barber's big pole and its eternal spiral.

"Here so early... cows already milked?"

And Alcide sits down in the chair, cracks the big smile of a big man who already has most of his day's work behind him, because that is the way of the world, by God. He is not the village barber-philosopher, nor a plumber at home with his feet up, waiting for the pipes to burst in some house, nor a housewife who hasn't a thing to do but a little housework before noon!

"Ah, Louis! Sometimes, those damn cows!..."

And if he does not finish, it's for one of three reasons. Maybe it's the towel the barber puts around his neck that cuts his sentence short. Or then again, maybe Alcide has nothing more to say about the cows, the

ONE BEAUTIFUL DAY TO COME

cow-shed, the milk and the early morning routine. Or perhaps, and maybe most of all, it's because for him as for everyone, complaining would lead nowhere. Every slightly drawn-out complaint turns into bitter and definitive words like "I would send it all packing and leave for the sun somewhere, live out my life with it." And one never knows with whom or what, in the end. So, better to leave the beginning of the complaint floating in the air and not say out loud words that make silences difficult, afterwards.

"Cut, cut! Don't hold back, all that damn hair makes my head itch when we get them big heat waves!"

And Louis, his comb in one hand, his scissors in the other, cuts away. His discreet smile beneath his discreet mustache in the big mirror in front of Alcide is an invitation to talk, or to get all worked up, or yet again, to rest.

The row boat is rocking a little. Not because the current is strong, however. Germain, sitting on the stern, both feet in the water, fishing pole under thigh and back to the sun, is making the boat tilt. Germain thinks, "Ah! Water, refreshing water, cold at first and then warm a bit later." And right after that, he thinks "Ah! To be with a woman, cool at first and then hot a bit later!" Suddenly, shivers dance over his back, currents climb wave after wave up to the nape of his neck. Shivers unknowable because nameless and nameless because unknowable. And vice versa once more. Shivers which he feels and lets himself feel, happy and endlessly surprised. "A cat," thinks Jacob, "my friend is a big cat that the sun unfolds like it unfolds the new leaves at the tip of the branches! Look at him! If a fat pike bit right now, took his bait, he would leap to his knees, easily, eyes alert, dip net ready, his left hand as skilled as his right and yet each performing different tasks at the same time, and he would land it, the wriggling pike, and he would have that smile that hurts me and relieves me, that smile of his that makes me feel empty and a little sad like when you've lost something precious."

But, for the moment, the line, with all its weights, stagnates and drifts at the whim of the current. The lead stirs about a little, brushing against bottom-loving algae, the anchor, or the back of a well-fed, uninterested rock bass. And Germain cradles himself by rocking the boat, his back to the sun and his thoughts, as they're called, wander precisely to somewhere the cats have curves of white skin, silky hair and graceful movements so human, so feminine and magnificent. Just like the river, at times.

The sun is now no longer that red ball which Big Gilles saw thrusting through the pines. Above the trees clawing at it, it has become pure light, it illuminates the sky, blinding if you look at it too much. So you lower your eyes. The forest steams right to its very edge as the shadows create caverns that will not long keep their black, mossy mysteries. The ferns imprison the night's dew in the funnel-shaped hollow of their leaves. But at the top of the great oaks, the thirst of the broad, precocious leaves will not be quenched before nightfall. Green deepening with every minute, green changing so quickly and needing so much sunlight that it is always thirsty, and its entire life is that thirst, that brilliance.

Big Gilles, the Métis, is walking cautiously, trying not to mutilate anything of this new life emerging from the dead leaves, last year's compost. This irrepressible life ever renews itself, growing, as they say. He presses on, placing his steps carefully, hesitating, his everyday pace now, towards the spring. He hears it murmuring against the rock, and yet the spring is still far off, beyond the fir trees. There is still the hillock, the fairies' hollow, iridescent water spurting from the rock. And Big Gilles thinks, "Each passing second counts, the world is never the same, you must open your eyes and nostrils wide, everything changes so quickly! Already, the blue sky is fading, the lake's emerging from the mist, the smell of sand's starting to weaken, the smell of spruce sap's stronger. If I'm trembling, this morning, it is not from old age but from the eternal youthfulness of this ancient planet. And because I am still here to see and know. I am not searching for the secrets like those people down there, in the village. It's the secrets that seek and find me. If their world of schools, churches, and town halls collapsed, if we suddenly found ourselves back at the beginning, who would know how to track the prey, set traps, walk by starlight, follow the wind, overcome the cold, survive? The air they breathe comes out of others' stove pipes. The air I breathe is pure and from the source. On the one hand that's good, but on the other bad – since this purity is paid for with solitude and despair..."

A branch cracked under his foot. Everyone has the right to get distracted, even Big Gilles. Exulting sometimes makes you lose track of things. Quickly, very quickly the squirrel has scurried up the tree. It is already half-way up, hanging on firmly, and it looks at Big Gilles as if to say, "I never hear you coming, you, never realize you are there until the last second, prowling, sighing behind me, close, too close to my worried fur."

The heat is rising, or maybe it's falling? In the white house, the kettle is whistling. Malvina rises She pauses for a moment in the garden. The earth lies untilled, the gladiola and dahlia bulbs are still in the cold and the dark, in the depths of the cellar. "I don't have the heart for flowers," she thinks and the thought which comes over her is not even sad, but abandoned, like after life. The kettle's screaming in the kitchen. Make the coffee. Perform, one after the other, the gestures of some sort of survival. With that void in her heart that renders eyes, arms and legs derisory. That void which deprives the body of its former beauty and grace. She slowly climbs the big veranda staircase. She stops. She looks at her hand on the banister. A weary hand which must, however, make the effort to hold, to mix, to cook, to wash, to pick, to scrub. The hand of empty days. Hand of a vague terror. Humiliated hand which is going to grow old, all alone. Malvina totters on the stairs. The kettle is whistling, screaming, calling, and something tears deep within Malvina, tears yet a bit more. "Is it the envelope of the soul," she says to herself, "already crumbling with sorrow?" And, immediately afterwards, she replies, "I want, nevertheless! I want so much! What's wrong with me, who am I to frighten people so much, to receive nothing, never, giving and giving and then it goes away, into a vacuum, this unwanted love?"

Brusquely, charged with that sharp anger that comes when your heart unknowingly fights fear, Malvina enters the kitchen, takes the kettle off the stove, pours the boiling water into the coffeepot. "An old maid is still a maid, a woman, and maybe that's what scares them, a woman, just a woman who loves and who is going to grow old?" Bitter, her coffee. She goes to drink it by the window. And yet, never in her old maid's memory has there been a more beautiful day!

Turning around, Malvina notices the letter on the table, propped against the empty flower vase, the one with the little blue cat on its plump side. (That vase! I'll break it, some morning when I'm stubborn and insolent.) Vina sits down facing the letter, her head in her palms, she sighs "They're arriving today, the newly-weds, it's really true!" It's frightful how much that word hurts: newly-weds.

They are kneeling down. Waiting. Their lips are murmuring and it is as if you could hear a fly, just one, buzzing in the church. In the sanctuary, the big lamp burns, eternal, and yet, the slightest gust of wind, if the window were to open...

But no. They protect the eternity of the sanctuary lamp. They need its little flame of the Holy Spirit. Hence, the windows do not open. The church is cool and dark, like an undergrowth, but with very different scents, much less troubling for our poor fragile senses, our senses slowed down by winter and by mornings of fasting. Their veils hide their gaze. Eyes turned inwards, eyes which do not mirror the soul but watch it, keep an eye on it. The first little nun is completely given over to divine love, and it is almost a sleepiness, and her head bends forward, bends until it touches the prie-dieu. But she resists, she straightens up, blinks her eyelids, divine love requires a firm determination, she must remain alert and endure a little suffering in her knees, it is good for that terrible pride. The second sister is busy calming her stomach, which is singing its own hymns and clearly has the right to do so, poor thing, but not so loud, not so loud! As for the third nun, she remembers her dream from the night before. A big horse with a warm muzzle gently worrying her, breathing deeply down her neck. Perhaps the horse of that half-breed, Big Gilles, that handsome idler who hasn't been coming to church any more since... since... And then she shivers with pleasure and is annoyed at herself for not being annoyed at herself for shivering like that.

27

When the priest finally comes in, softly coughing, his lace-fringed alb quivering like a wedding dress on the waxed tile floor, followed by his sleep-numbed altar boy, the sisters rise up, all three of them together, and it's then they clearly see that summer has really arrived, since they are alone at mass and that not even the cantor, Mr. Latour, has gotten out of bed this morning. Alone? No. Rachel Bédard is there, in the last pew, upright like an Easter statue. Rachel has paid for this mass for her late husband's soul. "Poor Léopold, who is still in purgatory, if not in hell which wouldn't surprise me, he loved another from down around the cove, a native, and hung himself in his barn, Lord Jesus, let us pray for him and for her!"

I am experiencing a most extraordinary passion deep within my nothingness. A passion of will and desire. A spirit before body, a violent surge, fierce desire to go through time, to cross the border between worlds, an irresistible desire for destiny. You must not think I am only waiting. I am not waiting: I am rhythm, I am liquid, I am fleeting, I am swift, I am on my way. Luminous, blazing, inevitable. I already sense the colour and taste of the trees: pines, maples, oaks, thrusting leaves, smooth flows of sap, seasons beyond here, promises! I can vaguely make out the bursts of light, and the shadows, the reflections, the mirages, all those beautiful traps to come. I already detect the sounds, the songs, the groans, the release, the pleasure, the salty tears, the sorrow, the delay of things and the impatience, desire, again, like now. Oh, it's so vast, so vague, so big! I cannot say: it's this and again that, since it is already something else and otherwise. Everything is moving so fast! The world spreads out, unfolds, flies off and curls up anew in a ball, deep within me, and starts off again. Faces, arms, body odours, how I miss you! I am too abstract, too abrupt, too carried away.

Imagine a dewdrop full of the desire to quench the many thirsts of plants, and that flees in the wind, that loses itself in a raging sky, flying in the storm, not knowing where it will end up, in what corolla, what leaflet, nor even whether it will not simply evaporate: that's me, my love. And perhaps, also, it is already the child inside you.

In the sky, a big cloud, just one, rolls in the wind, gliding like a mis-shapen balloon. It resembles something or someone, but what, or whom? The cloud keeps changing and it is disconcerting, that big white shape, familiar and unknown, moving through the village sky. There, you see! The cloud stops, with its vast shadow, above the big hill. What's more, you can hear something in the echo of the hill. What is it? Sparkling, as though the road was crumbling or a shower of stones set it crackling. It's the hooves of Big Gilles' horse. The animal and its rider are going down to the village. Their pure nonchalance, in the white light of full day, is dazzling and disturbing. The big half-breed, his legend, the strange things said about him and his horse: proud, too proud, both of them. He poaches in the village woods. He has neither hearth nor home, always deep in the forest, or else on the dusty roads fleeing the village, wandering no one knows where, like a scoundrel ancestor returned from the ancient barbarian world. Dashing, solitary, with a very disturbing smile, teeth worn out but radiant, barely recognizable, like some resuscitated *coureur des bois,* a riddle to all.

They take Francois-Xavier Road, the one that leads to the lake through the middle of the village. He is going to pass right by the white house in a moment. And Big Gilles is going to ceremoniously raise his large felt hat to salute you, whoever you are, you or your shadow on the shore, or else the frogs or the water lilies or yet again the terns diving into the waves like swords in pursuit of silver minnows. He salutes, that's all. But it is grandiose, threatening, perhaps. "The thing is, he looks far and deep, Big Gilles does." That too is said, amongst the rumours that halo him, and that talent slightly hurts the ordinary in each of us. Who, unflinching, can confront that hawk-like gaze?

The silhouette – Big Gilles on his parading horse – slowly, very slowly disappears without totally fading in the full daylight creating a kind of haze now, around so-called inanimate things. A vision. This summer's first. The poor priest: it is not his fault but, in these parts, church is not where you see visions.

Louis has turned the knob of the old radio that has been in the corner of what he calls his "living room," since... my God, since forever. It squeaks, it crackles and then a voice bursts forth and a few violins too. This female voice, a rasping, painful yet proud voice lingers in the room, bumps against the walls, along the mirrors, crosses, climbs, rebounds, comes back towards the two men, then returns to haunt the big mirror which now reflects two emotional faces. So this voice does not flee, it cannot escape them, remains imprisoned by the barber shop and Louis and Alcide's unwavering attention. They have stopped talking, they are listening to the voice which is overwhelming and yet somehow seems natural:

Quand il me prend dans ses bras
Qu'il me parle tout bas
Je vois la vie en rose

When he takes me in his arms
and he whispers to me
Life is like a dream

And then – oh but it's almost imperceptible! Alcide succumbs to the enchantment. The voice has crossed the slightly foggy, familiar zones, it has found his heart beneath the wads of seasons survived as best one could, and naturally Alcide is dreaming about happiness, in other words about Theresa, his wife, and his gaze moistens in the big mirror.

"And to say that I don't know how, I've never really known how to tell her how much I love her, she who always waits without that down-in-the-mouth look of women who wait...." The song is searching deep down inside Alcide, and unearths images of warm summers, of orchards in bloom, of horseback rides in the snow, of bonfires by the buckwheat field, of Theresa, very young with her desire, her need to be happy, "my wife, my only love, ill-loved, my beautiful, patient, courageous Theresa." Louis smiles, his refined mustache stretches out above his slender lips. Louis knows exactly where the voice has gone and in what tender flesh Alcide has received it. Louis knows this voice by heart and he discreetly, softly, hums along with it. Louis knows that the singer's rasping voice has become for Alcide the voice of the wife one forgets through always having her there, close to you, attentive, unobtrusive, the gentle presence which, alas! a man takes for granted. "You and your music Louis!" and they both smile in the big mirror and they know, but do not say, why such a voice enters the mundane, everyday world when, strangely, the heart is again fragile, enchanted by the beginning of summer that is imperceptibly melting away the ancient harshness of winter. And perhaps this is as it should be, after all, since we must melt once in a while anyway, and feel that there are still some things left to do to change, to see life like a dream, a little bit. And Alcide thinks, "She loves picnics so much and talks, oh rarely but still, about a trip to see her dear old friend, Janette, in Virginia in the United States, on the seashore. And then too, there are the little things that we loved doing together, in the beginning. On coming back from the big meadow, we would stretch out under the apple trees and I would put my head on her stomach and then she would say to me, 'Alcide do you hear the song of the wind in the branches? That wind is my early childhood.' And she would talk of times before me, by the great river, of her brothers going off on the water, of winters that were too long, of learning to wait, that beautiful, hard-to-master quality women have, and then she would move her fingers through my hair so that, for a few touching seconds, time would weigh on us less heavily. Yes," thinks Alcide, "if we really want to, we can experience them together again, those everyday things and words that contain eternity."

Louis looks at Alcide in the big mirror: "You do not think that your hair is too short do you, Alcide?" "No, no and anyways, it grows back so fast!" The tall man gets up, rubs his itchy nape and brushes himself off: mysteriously, he is happy. Just like every time he comes to get his hair cut at Louis' barber shop.

Everywhere, except maybe in the heart of the forest, there is this haze of light in the air, this glistening of the air itself. The sun is mixed up in all that, so the village shines as though it had a halo. The roof of the church splatters like hot coals, like volcano lava in those pictures in Life magazine that we look through at Louis' barber shop while awaiting our turn in the chair, the nights before big parties in the village. The tree tops, even those we trim on Main Street, are thrust, sunk deep into the liquid, burning blue of the sky. The slightest silhouette of people, animals, objects, even insects is doubled by its shadow and everyone takes the mystery for granted. We manage as best we can with this strange splitting in two. That's the way things are. A black ghost follows or precedes you wherever you go. That's the bother, like a sort of price to pay for having so much beautiful light on earth. And anyway, that shadow is cool, and without it, would we not explode in this absolute light?

Only the mechanic's dog is forever surprised by this black dog, strangely stretched out, spiteful, which he can neither flee nor frighten by biting into it with hearty, useless rage. He runs in vain, circling himself, stretched out full length on the grass; nothing works. The black dog runs with him, turns with him and stretches out with him full length on the grass. Fortunately, the mechanic's dog is neither too sharp nor too intelligent, and does not persist. Very quickly he forgets about his ghost and falls asleep. He is, as we say, a good mutt. He never sleeps long, for there are too many exciting smells in the fields he hunts in. Having forgotten his shadow, the other black dog, he gets back up, preparing to follow a track, an exasperating smell, a hot little taste in the grass. If he turns around he glimpses the black dog following him as though to steal his prey. But suddenly he takes off again in pursuit of the smell, and he forgets. The shadow, however, catches up to him just as he is passing under the fence that separates the fields from the main road. Then he crouches in the ditch, he growls, he shows his teeth. But the black dog has disappeared. In its place, enthroned on one of the fence posts, is the orange cat, taunting him. The shadow is forgotten for the rest of the day: the orange cat has reappeared.

You are sleeping. Strange, you do not look at all fragile when you sleep. You do not open your mouth like most sleepers, who appear to be seeking death. You remain vibrant, you do not change, you are not absent. You are resting. One of your shoulders gleams in the light of my lamp reaching you at the same time as the ink-covered papers, my hand, my daydreams, the book. It is night, holding you in its hand like a gentle ogre. It is night, holding me in its fist of blood. I continue, my love. In fact, I am reaching the beginning of everything: I am going to summon here, in the middle of the clearing – this halo trembling slightly around my hands – that man and that woman, my origins, my headwaters, my world before life. You will see their superb pose come alive, burst from this frame in which you met them. You will see them love each other shamelessly, alone together, in that world before us, that sad world where they were like two islands on a big, bitter lake.

Elsewhere, in another village which is not my village, on the other side of the lake, even further beyond the mountains, on the steps of a church similar to all beautiful village churches, my father and mother are standing alone, smiling, hugging each other, motionless. But there is no photographer, no uncle nor cousin waving a camera. However, they do not budge. It is their wedding day, the day of their deliverance. Gertrude is no ordinary bride, and Maurice is not a bridegroom like any other. The bells are ringing very discreetly – for they are getting married "against their families' wishes," as the expression goes. They are eager to leave their petty town, its sadness, its shame, and to go away to the other village, to live their life which will not be easy, as they well know, but it will not be hell and that's better than nothing.

Gertrude throws her bride's bouquet without aiming. Made of red lilies, of trillium from the undergrowth, very ordinary spring flowers: as I have told you, Gertrude is no ordinary bride. A pretty bouquet that says their good-byes, that goes forth to bring luck to the birds, and will not be in the family album either.

And me, I am there between them, like a ferment in their blood. They kiss with their mouths open, and in their saliva, in their joy, in the bright sunshine on their skin, I am present, already.

They put out their tongues, all three of them together. The altar boy makes sure that the gold paten does not tickle their chins because they would jump and then Jesus would no longer be able to melt in peace in their mouths, sliding saintly down their throats, avoiding their teeth, as is proper. They lower their heads, all three of them together, and they feel, they truly feel, Resurrection, radiant, with its good wheat taste, going down into their stomachs. Then they get up, all three of them together, at peace, their cornets perfectly straight, their large wooden rosaries striking against their stiff skirts. Oh! Jesus, gentle and humble of heart!

Rachel Bédard, they notice out of the corner of their eye, all three of them together, has not come up to receive communion. She is sitting with her head in her hands and you can very distinctly hear her sobs and the echo of her sobs in the peaceful church. The priest, who is, after all, on his home turf in his church, squints, looks at Rachel Bédard over the top of his glasses, coughs, coughs again, and in a deliberately loud voice he says, "Rachel, come by the vestry after mass, I have to have a word with you!"

The first one truly jumped. The second one opened her eyes wide, eyes still filled with heavenly bliss. The third uttered an "Ah!" of surprise, of emotion, of compassion, you never know with her. Rachel has not stopped crying, her face in her hands, "Oh! Jesus, gentle and humble of heart."

"Get the net in, Jacob, for God's sake! Get it in I'm telling you!"

The walleye is wriggling, about to get away. Germain does what he can to haul the fish up into the row-boat but it is up to Jacob to manoeuvre his net. If Germain gives his fishing rod the slightest jerk, the walleye's cheek, delicate as silk paper, will tear, and the fish will dive head first and will disappear very quickly, like lightning, to the bottom. It's a nice catch, it must weigh eight or ten pounds and that is just why Jacob is paralyzed. "Never saw a fish like this before! Big as, long as..."

"Hurry Jacob, you idiot, the net, we're going to lose it!"

But Jacob is dreaming, dumbfounded, and the precious seconds pass, fatally. It would be hard to say what exactly it is that prevents Jacob from hurrying, but it just may be sheer wonder, pure and simple. A kind of shock, too much glistening beauty just beneath the surface, and then the anticipation of the story-telling, that suffocating joy with which Jacob, this evening, on the wharf, will relate the enchantment of silver and gold, the big walleye, and Germain's wild eyes as he was pulling it up gently towards the row-boat. Time has suddenly stopped, intense, like biting heat in the chest, like paralysis. The eternal side and the fugitive side of this extraordinary moment, the sudden blinding precision of the landscape, the sky too blue, too empty, the bulrushes swaying in the wind, as if nothing special was happening, the anchor cable plunging to the dark bottom, and on the water, the sharply delineated shadow of a seagull in flight; all that in the same exhausting second and his arm that wants to move, that is going to move, stretch, grasp the net, triumph over lethargy, yes, the net.

"Damn fool! Jacob, what got into you?"

"What got into me," Jacob thinks, "what got into me? But Germain, don't you see, we were dreaming! A fish like that just can't exist, you know it, we were dreaming, Germain!"

When it is warmer, in July, I will take you to the end of the world. Meaning where the town road stops and where a stand of wild raspberry bushes begins, and beyond it are the fields left in fallow because the Indians burn them each time someone tries to sow them. A steppe of shrivelled trees spreads out, endlessly. When Maurice drove me there for the first time, I was five years old, and I remember thinking, "This is the end of the world." I found it frightening, yet beautiful that the world should stop at the end of the road, that emptiness, abyss, death should begin just beyond the raspberry patch. That meant the catechism was right: an end really and truly existed, heaven or hell, a limit to our adventure. It was as though I had always known, without wanting to, that we were not immortal, that we were fragile and that we must hasten to love, run, discover the earth, enjoy the world on this side of the raspberry bushes. Beyond them, ferocious beasts await us, to feast upon our ephemeral flesh. Big Gilles will laugh mightily at my fear, which he will define as a crazy little Catholic's nightmare. Even now, when I juggle with a bottomless problem, some-

ONE BEAUTIFUL DAY TO COME

times, especially at night, I dream about that stand of wild raspberry bushes, the ultimate boundary, the final point, beyond which life stops and the
inconceivable, nothingness, emptiness begins.

We shall sit down in the grass, both of us, in the shade, and savour
the mauve, sweet raspberries. We shall make love, perhaps, with the
bees buzzing around us. We shall feel death very close by but unaware
of us, of our bodies hidden behind the grasses.

Childhood gleams between us now like a halo. We are likewise
haunted by it, triumphant both. Just a little more and we shall tumble
together into a happiness I stubbornly believed was too simple for us.
And then, the child will come.

Big Gilles has dismounted from his horse. He jumped to the ground
like a cowboy, easily, and the horse, used to it, did not budge.

"Belle-Fille, my best, my beauty!"

The mare accepts the compliment with modesty, not even raising
her head to him. Gilles undoes the knot tying up the big leather bag that
was quivering a moment ago against Belle-Fille's flank. He opens it: the
little red fox is motionless, curled up at the bottom of the bag. The
Métis thrusts his hand in, grabbing the animal by the scruff of its neck.

"Come, my treasure, come and see the great weather!"

The little fox barely opens its eyes. Like a flash, it goes to curl up in
the hollow of Big Gilles' left armpit, there where a familiar scent will protect it. When the Métis enters the forest shadows, the fox raises its head,
sniffs, and comes to perch himself like a crow on the man's shoulder,
attentive, completely reassured. The first trap they visit is empty and the
fox peers sidelong at its master as though to say, "There are sneakier ones
than I, the eldest, the most beautiful, you will not trick them easily!"
Judging from the way the shadows of the birch trees are stretched out
over the carpet of pine needles, it is barely nine o'clock, and Big Gilles has
all the time in the world today, like yesterday, like tomorrow, like always.

You are sleeping in the hammock gently rocking you on the veranda of the big white house. That house we entered after Vina died, my

aunt had left as it was, had not even changed the quilt bedspread in the bright room. All those years! For her, for me, for you, a different sort of time has passed. Yesterday, after supper, you asked me,

"You wouldn't be writing that book if we hadn't both come live in this house, right?"

And I answered, "Probably not. Another one, for sure, I cannot help but write, but not this one." But I thought, I imagined, when I started the book, that I would link, mix, record their existences with mine and perhaps, even if it is unreasonable, obtain forgiveness for the distance, my insensitivity, the cruelty of my adolescence. And then we wanted the child right away. As soon as you smelled the lake air, the lilac, the good sun dust in this bedroom where I was born, the child was with us. And this again, my love, this that I do not understand but which trembles deep within me and demands the book: forgetting is useless. That nomadic, fast-paced, blinded life, so far from happiness and attentiveness, my life as hypnotized disciple, of red wine, my life of city and will-power did not distance me from the white house, on the contrary. I felt trapped, I flew against the walls, an absurd bird thirsting for sky and amnesia. I haunted the bright room, an obsessed ghost with broken feathers.

Perhaps, my love, childhood does not set us free until we come eat in its hand, docile, defeated, unbound?

Malvina is re-reading the letter to be quite sure. Even if she has already read it twelve times, the letter still hurts and delights her.

May 14, 1946
My dear cousin,

If only you knew how eager Maurice and I both are to arrive! Are you sure that the house will be big enough to take us both in, my husband and me? You are so kind, how can I ever manage to thank you, for goodness' sake? Malvina, how I love this man! And you know the endless trouble I had to get him as my own, and give myself to him! We dream of a simple life, and we'll help you around the house, I do promise that. Maurice will soon find work, he is so resourceful. As for me, I am no stranger to house-work and am certainly not considered a lazybones, you know it.

Oh dear, dear Vina, my dear cousin, may the good Lord bless you for being so generous! Heaven help us be worthy of your kindness. So, we get married Monday, June 2, and we arrive the same day, in the evening, in Maurice's old jalopy which will no longer have any wedding decorations, for you know how very simple this wedding will be. Our poor families, if they knew how we pity them from the heights of our happiness, and if they knew how much they have hurt us nonetheless! But no one, never ever ever will remove from my finger that ring Maurice will put on it. Oh, how I love him and how sure I am of him and certain of myself, Vina! I'll tell you all about it when we talk, in the evening, on the veranda of the big white house.

With all my love and many, many thanks,
Your First Cousin, Gertrude

P.S. Give Sam a big hug and tell him we love him too. Your Samuel is so proud and kind, dear Vina. He is a man to be loved, that's for sure!

A man to be loved, Sam-the-Wanderer? A man to forget, rather, to lose somewhere in the vast memory of unhappy seasons. An absent man, a man who left, staggering, wild-eyed, collar turned up: "Sam, the dreamer, flee-ing, my love left for wherever yet again and, I fear, this time for good."

Malvina is quietly crying. Her tears are sliding smoothly, running along her nose and raining down about that very letter, landing pre-cisely on those words: "How sure I am of him and certain of myself, Vina!" Then she sponges the letter with the hem of her apron, folds it in two, then in three, then in four and puts it back in its place which is right out in the open, against the flower pot full of red trillium, in the middle of the kitchen table. "At least that makes two happy people," thinks Vina, "two who won't live on mirages and fraying dreams. And that's something, at least, in this life of misery!"

The cat has jumped onto the convent fence post. Proud statue, it stares at the dog below. Its fur is haloed with beautiful russet gold, because of the sun behind. In vain the dog jumps, exhausts himself against the post, yelps, nearly has a stroke; he is not bothering the cat in the slightest, busy as it is contemplating the light, inhaling the morning smells, inventing its thousand-and-first story to avoid boredom, today again. It is a handsome, indolent, russet prince, haughty and melancholic, perched upon its favourite post, shimmering with light and mocking the mechanic's dog, for variety, to keep busy, to while away sluggardly time.

In the sixth trap visited, a hare is still twitching, black blood in its beige fur. Big Gilles gently collects it, frees the animal's paw. The hare does not complain, save with its eyes. But perhaps that is simply its hare's gaze, its way of seeing man, that stranger. A black storm of pupils, half pain, half rage. Not by the ears, as do barbarians, but by the scruff of the neck, the big Métis catches the hare, calmly caresses it, then puts it in the bag. "Another one who will live with me a few days, a few nights, long enough to see that I'm decent company, no matter what they say in the village! Right, Ti-Fox?" The little fox, drawn by Gilles voice and warm breath, comes and sniffs at the bag, then returns to nest in the hollow of the giant's armpit, where the scent of trust is like nowhere else.

A few moments ago, children came to play on the beach, drawn by our dog. They were wearing orange and blue raincoats. You went out to greet them, talk with them; I watched you through the bedroom window. Immediately, they surrounded you, I could hear their easy, flowing laughter, and your own clear, untamed laugh. You threw a stick in the water and the dog dove in, fast. The children were shouting, hopping on the little wharf. Then, you turned around, probably you had guessed I was at the window. You smiled at me without seeing me. Your hair in the wind, one hand shading your eyes, for a long while you looked towards the window. I stayed there, on my elbows, dumbfounded. That was how I imagined you before we met, and, back then, I used to think,

"Old buddy, you're dreaming, you're afraid, you're shrivelling up, you're hurting, it's bitterness that's making you invent this woman, you're getting old, you're bitter..." I moved my arms to open the window, slowly, savouring my joy. I waved at you, you and the children, and in my head I could hear your voice repeating the words you said to me, the first evening: "I like only innocence, and you must not think it is just an unhealthy continuation of childhood. Neither is it some naivete protected by blindness. It is a leap outside oneself and very few are still able to make it, I'm talking about adults, of course. You, yes, you can. You're capable of that natural, peaceful attention, you're lucky..."

I return to the book, the misty words trembling before my eyes. I have left the window open, I want to continue the book with the music of your laughter, below. Everything outdated and fierce in me has melted, thanks to you, my love. Melts a little more, day by day.

The priest has taken on his soft voice, approximately soft. Rachel Bédard is holding her scarf over her eyes, her nose, her mouth. The sacristy smells of just-snuffed candles, cold incense, and obedience. Through the tall windows, an ancient-looking sun pierces the curtains and makes the floor tiling shine too brightly, like the light on miracle scenes in catechism pictures. The mood is solemn, imposing, sad.

"Have to get a hold on yourself, my daughter. Think of your children!"

She sniffles, Rachel Bédard does, in her scarf, and the echo of her sniffling exasperates the walls of the most dignified sacristy, too dignified for the chagrin of weeping widows.

"You just can't understand. I do love my children. I give them all I have, they're managing fine, but me! Dishonour, unhappiness! What that man did, nobody, not even me, deserved that!"

"Now, now..."

Soft, ambiguous little pats on Rachel Bédard's shoulder blade, honey and warmth in the priest's voice, derision in his winy breath, fetid consolation. In other words, nothing. Nothing to calm Rachel Bédard's dismay, her pain. Nothing to replace the former confidence, the former pride, when the village was blissfully unaware of the sins of one Léopold, her husband, her deceased: his rutting with the wanton squaw, in the cove. "On beds, never the same, of spruce branches, cedar, and even on the soft moss in the undergrowth, in the always-empty communal fields, in the wind, the sun, he, my husband, with her, the Indian, both laughing with pleasure. And I surprised them, that's the worst part! Together, mad laughter cascading, their bodies mingled, naked, and so far from their clothing, a hundred feet away in the grass. Their carefreeness, and then his violence when he came back home, straw in his hair. His sick eyes, already lost, I knew it."

She has suddenly risen and is running like a freed animal, running across the too-shiny tiles of the holy sacristy, a shadow fleeing too much light and, on the threshold, she turns around, puts her scarf back on her head and shouts, "He killed himself, Father! That's my shame, and you don't care a bit, just like the others, full of the Lord though you be!"

"Now come, my child..."

She does not say, "Don't say another word, Father, That's enough, quite enough, I have to carry my pain further, the house, the day to get through..." But she does look at the priest with her pride-stripped, humility-stripped servant's eyes, and she flees. The priest bobs his head, as powerless as God himself.

The row boat is drifting. Germain lets his feet drag in the water where they make two ripples into which sunshine flows like molten gold. Jacob is still holding the anchor at arm's length, bent over to look at the bottom, noticing the grasses and rocks. But Germain will not signal him just yet. He has other plans. The mother-of-pearl little beach, the one with willow branches over it, like a billionaire's beach umbrella, over there, beside the big point. To stretch out there, what a joy! "The sand will be cool, it'll smell of bulrushes, algae, willing woman," Germain thinks. Have a nap there, smell all those scents that make you drunk and feel the velvet flower of a woman dream opening in your belly.

"He's leading me on," thinks Jacob, "and he's enjoying the mystery, as we drift, my continual astonishment, the big cat my cousin is amused by my tender feelings for him, by my obedience, and he's not being mean, no, cats aren't mean. But he can't help it, he needs all his strength, always. It's that great confidence, beneath his skin, that he listens to and that makes him happy and makes me stupid with the weight of the anchor at arm's length and the hot sun beating down on me."

Simply by following the current, the boat comes to rest on the sandy shallows. Over there, on the beach, a big heron is beating its long, slow wings that look so heavy. It takes off, grazes the water, slowly soars up. How is it going to climb into the air with that tranquil, unenthusiastic movement? It looks like a man imitating a bird. And yet, slowly, the big heron with the impossible wings reaches the sky. It is already over the point and its shadow, even slower than it, lands in the water, glides over the water, like an airplane reaching the sky without moving its wings.

Germain has jumped. His feet sink into the golden sand shimmering on the bottom.

"Pull up the canoe, Jacob, we're going to rest for a while!"

And Jacob puts down the anchor, tears himself away from the heron's flight and comes to haul the boat up onto the beach while his cousin, the big cat, dives in, screaming like... a cat.

On a country road, beside an alfalfa field, the old Buick has come to a stop. The radio is playing and the driver's door is open, but there is no one in the car. From the road, you can see a little island of cedar in the middle of the field, not very far from the road. Shade for the cows, or perhaps a summer oasis for the farmer. There they are, both of them. Maurice has taken off his jacket, his too-tight tie, his sticky shirt. Bare-chested, he is leaning against a big branch and watching her: his wife, Gertrude, who is sitting very straight in her luminous dress, on an old stump, her hair almost red because a ray of sun is falling exactly on her as though to show the world her perfect innocence and her pure desire for this man staring at her with a smile. In my father's eyes, there is a troubled look, a welling up of tears too long held back. Suddenly, he plunges towards her, he wants to sink his head in her belly. My mother caresses his back, his hair, and my father cries, he cannot stop. "There, there, we are together, my love," she says. He says, "I'm rumpling your whole dress."

She thinks: "Good Lord, rumple, rumple! I beg you, don't hold back any longer, my husband. For months now you've been swallowing sideways, touching me with your eyes only. Give me your hands, your mouth! From a distance only, at church, at the market, you've desired me, unable to say anything, unable to do anything for months! I love you for having waited, like a horse in a corral, I know your ardour. In a few hours, we'll be at the big white house, my love, it's scarcely believable!"

He stays there, on his knees, his head in her dress, close to her belly where I am already half alive. He moans, he has her two willing hands on his shoulders, he is completely sheltered. "How beautiful his shoulders are, a freed man's," Gertrude thinks. Through the branches come a few notes of a song playing on the old Buick's radio, floating with the breeze.

Comme au premier jour, toujours, toujours
Je me souviendrai du jour
Où sous le cerisier
Le coeur brisé, tu m'as parlé d'amour...

Like that first day, always, forever
I shall remember the day
When under the cherry tree
Heart-broken, you spoke to me of love...

Their hearts are in their throats. They are married. They are free!

You set the pages down on your knees and you ask me: "But why are Gertrude and Maurice fleeing? What have they done wrong?" I look at you with my calm eyes in which you have long known how to read my fears, my burgeonings. Then you begin to guess. You rise, you hug the pages with one arm and, with the other, you pick up the little frame with their picture. I can see that you immediately recognize on their faces the fever signs. An old fever I have inherited. That sort of banked ardour, mute passion, lack of virtue, of hypocrisy, of calculation in their eyes, on their skin, that veiled radiance, and also that terror. You kiss me. The pages, crushed between us, get rumpled during the kiss. After, I simply say, "Imagine, it was thirty-seven years ago!" And you imagine, easily. The fear, cowardice and violence of their families, the atrocious zeal of others. That rape, always, of fleshly innocence, that stoning, the sin of loving with one's sovereign body, that flight beyond God, that sacrilege, that outrage. You revisit, in thought, your mutilated loved ones: bitter old maids; drunken uncles; teenagers driven from paradise; absurd, desperate, mute grooms and brides. For an hour, panting, overwhelmed, you re-discover them, all those accurst relatives. The massacre of the holy Innocents which has never ceased. You blush from that powerful vision. You talk, you talk and they emerge from times ancient, flayed, pathetic, alive!

We must flee, my love. Remember us in the beginning, how we almost caused a scandal. Our friends, our families tried so hard to stop this love they feared. We must flee, my love, because we frighten them. Otherwise, we'll be burned at the stake, massacred or smothered; in any case: death. You return the rumpled pages to me, you take my hand, put it on your stomach and say, "For her, or for him, things will be different."

They follow each other, resemble each other. Same hasty steps, same rubbing of soles, same dry rustling of skirts, same quick shadows on the road behind them. The first one hums as she trots along, proud to be leading the caravan, the single file, and she thinks: "Ah, we three, what a cheerful company to celebrate God and his grace!" And she nods, rocks and shakes her happy little nun's head, in love with her Eternal. The second is breathing deeply, filling her lungs with the clover and dew and fresh cedar of the convent hedge. As for the third, she has not yet raised her head, enraptured with the presence of the holy bread still warm deep down in her stomach and which she confuses with her soul, for her greater enchantment. She is thinking, "I am absolutely nothing, nothing compared to Him, nothing but a pusillanimous little nun under His sun."

Just as the first one stops to open the gate of the convent's kitchen entrance for discretion and humility, the second gives an enormous sneeze, no doubt due to the spicy scent of the peppermint. "Oh!" says the second, surprised. She was deep in meditation. She often meditates like that, and comes back to earth only when one or the other of the two other little nuns makes dry and shocking little noises. Then her eyes, immense, stunned, make the first and second laugh: her eyes look scandalized and are so very comical! "Hee! Hee! Hee!" they say, mockingly. Their shoulders rise and fall and their spastic shadows, on the convent lawn, in turn astonish the perched cat who wonders...

The storm that has been threatening us all day has finally passed by overhead. All we got was a heavy downpour, a loose net of big drops through which we could see the lake, the beach, the sky like a landscape on a scratchy film. You say you are hot, so I come close to you and breathe your sweat which smells so good, I get drunk on it, I slide along your body in the bed. The book will wait. I desire you so suddenly that you laugh, staring at me with your tall, surprised girl's gaze. You ask me not to penetrate you, you take my penis in your hand. You say you want to feel me streaming onto your fingers, your wrists. You say I taste of clover, salt and also almonds. You say, "To think it will be one of these minute, luminescent, opaque, mysterious moon-fish that will waken the egg in me. Taste! See how our child will be made of a perfume, an essence too!" And you laugh, holding your fingers out to me, your head thrown back, like a child having fun with the forbidden.

"The worst thing," thinks Vina, "is that he must be roaming around somewhere, not far away. Sobered up, Sam, full of remorse but stubborn, proud as the church steeple. I know he is hesitating to head down the highway and that he'll head down it anyway. Because he said he would and also because he thinks that's his destiny.

"Malvina, my dearest, what do you want, I can't help it, the damn bottle has got me on a leash! If I stay with you, it'll mean there'll be not just one but two zombies, in the long run. That's how it is, not to mention the itch to roam, the call of far-off places that will drive me crazy fit to be tied if I marry you and then we settle down in the big white house. And anyway, I'm too proud to endure the 'good citizens'' sarcasm, they're already talking about us as a silly couple, a somewhat well-to-do spinster and a lazy drunkard. No, no, Vina, I'd just as soon forget about it, hit the road, and let you get on with a decent life."

Decent? Malvina climbs the stairs with a pair of new sheets she had embroidered herself, dreaming about her own wedding. She caresses the slightly rough cloth, plunges her nose in it: it smells slightly of camphor, outdoors and especially lavender. "At least," she thinks, tearlessly and with nothing too broken in the grain of her inner voice – inevitably a frenzied voice, a voice that will eventually be able to speak of other matters, one day, the voice of survival and bitterness – "they'll serve Gertrude and Maurice well, my beautiful sheets, so smooth, drawn so tightly on the big bed, and I'll put lily petals on the pillows as my parents used to, poor dears, and I'll open the window so that the breeze perfumes the bed and I'll put the crucifix in the chest of drawers so that He, from high on His cross, will not stop those two from taking their time, savouring their wedding night, taking full advantage of it, it only happens once and even then not for everyone."

The big clock at the top of the stairs, where Malvina stops to catch her breath, chimes ten long chimes that go off to echo through the empty rooms of the big, sun-drenched white house.

"Good Lord, already ten o'clock!"

She could just as well have said: "Only ten o'clock!"

He has gotten tangled up in the barbed wire fence like a dislocated scarecrow. Poor dog, the cat has driven him crazy. He is frothing at the mouth, winded, his muzzle bleeding and flies whirling around his head. In his eyes is stupor at having let himself be made mad with anguish by that russet ball bouncing before him, driving him ill with rage. Like a flash, without his being able to give it a second's thought, he rushed forward, blind, furious. Brambleberry bushes, hedges, cedars flashed by beneath him as he became a bird, a hawk, an eagle. A brief halt at the foot of the cherry tree in front of the bank, where the cat was perching, then came the dive towards the yards, garbage cans toppling behind him, their clanging echoing in the lane behind the market and, finally, the cat stopped on top of a big motor oil drum. So, in a last burst, gathering his strength, the dog jumped, sure he'd grab it in his jaws this time, already crunching it, already salivating. But the cat – how the devil did it do it? – leaped, disappearing behind the market wall. The dog did see the fence, but too late. Suddenly he had it in his muzzle, in his teeth, and then there was a flash in his head, the red ending of a quick, burning illusion.

He is licking his suffering chops, salty with blood. As for the cat, it's looking at him from high on the crab apple tree. It's not even proud. It simply had fun, and then forgets about it. What a sunny day! How long it is, this day!

That little crab apple tree behind the house, Malvina, the one that, come autumn, will give its bright fruit, its blood red crab apples, fills with birds every morning, like a sanctuary. Your tree, your love tree, proud as a peacock's tail this morning, all its leaves already out. That little crab apple tree, Vina, is strong of faith. And then, it does not really need hope nor dreams to be born again, to perfume the air, to make love with the sunlight. That is unfair, eh Malvina? That strong, bitter sap deep in the heart of the branches and that mocks us with its senseless surge, burns us with its mad, inexhaustible flow. You stare at your tree and you sing

> *Sur la plus haute branche*
> *Le rossignol chantait...*
> *On the highest branch*
> *The nightingale was singing*

But this morning, on the highest branch of the little crab apple tree, a starling is squawking, and it is you, my love, who are singing.

In the fleeting light of childhood, all future apparitions are announced. Memory does its work, and then we forget, because one has to continue after all, learn, load up on meaning and reason. Later, we think we are imagining when an overwhelming love experience, or some special person, surges forth. Or simply an inexplicable good mood or anxiety. However, for those who, like me, have not managed to forget, some revelations are not revelations at all. I, for example, know that the spot mentioned in Rimbaud's *Bateau ivre*, "Sweeter than to children the flesh of tart apples, the green water penetrates my pine hull," is just a little upstream from Barque Isle, just where a very precise, very beautiful stand of bulrush grows, I'll take you, it is still there. All Mozart: such is autumn on the south slope of the mountain, where red oak, yellow birch and orange maples billow in the wind, you will see, it is symphonic, and truly Mozart. The perfect clarity of childhood make every new thing transparent. Each discovery is a memory and we fly to it, because we know. I am not talking about the abstract belief in an ideal world that childhood instills deep in us, instilled deep in me. It is the waiting that quickly becomes desire, some call it hope; it is that magic which will remember itself. On the beach, before the white house too soon left, in the mountains or yet again in the undergrowth around the village, I knew a thousand things that came to be. It can take five, ten or twenty years to come, but it comes. And it comes as it was foretold, thus desired, or feared. We are not the ones turning the wheel. We are the wheel. I know that you will laugh, or will smile, at least, on reading these words, my love. Yes, everything was in me, memory simply restores to me the enchantment.

Thus, you are this place on the beach, the exact spot where you yourself said, the first night: "Here, I can breathe, start breathing again." If I had not first met you here, I could not have led you here. You would have passed by, I would not have stopped you, we would not have fallen in love, we would not be making the child, nothing would exist today of that beautiful frenzy which surpasses us, carrying us forward like some enveloping wave. No: if, on seeing you, I had not seen the summer sky above us, the lake before us and the pines around us, I could not have believed it was you.

I recognize the power of a desire, its inevitability; I accept its tension, and submit to its delirium only if childhood appears in the images born from an encounter. And from you were born all images. They are resuscitated. I had forbidden them, I was crazed, lost, unplugged. The child coming will be born of these images, of my childhood and yours, rediscovered. Thus shall he come, and not otherwise.

Eleven o'clock on the post office clock in another village. Sam is hesitating. The post card is trembling in his fingers. His other hand is moist, deep in his pocket. Saying goodbye is hard, when you still have so much love in your breath. But it must be done. Open the mail box, slide in the card. "Finished, it's finished, I forget everything about her, forever. Her soft weight on my stomach, her hair in my neck, her intoxicating perfume, her calm like a little animal's, confident in me, everything! May she and her enchantments never reappear in my memory, nor my dreams, nor elsewhere in the world, ever."

Almost crazy with sadness and gnawed at by dull anger, Sam slipped the card into the box. It is on meeting the gaze of the post office lady that he realizes his memories of Vina can never be erased, will always be mixed in with the gleam of bottles, the mirages on the roads, endlessly sinking with him, like the ghost ships in his childhood pirate stories.

Frightened, he runs to his truck. The bottle awaits him, on the seat. He swallows a good glug of whisky that burns and pacifies him. To the bottle, he says, "I've chosen you, my Christ!" And he repeats the oath aloud, shouting in the truck. And then, the words written on the post card come dancing before his eyes, fatal, poisonous.

Vina,
I've never loved you. I am the meanest man in the country. You've got to forget me. Got to forgive me. Goodbye. Pray for me, Vina, I beg you.
Sam

On the other side of the card, a bouquet of wild flowers bursting with colour and which, nonetheless, is called a still life.

He is kissing her. She has flung her head against the seatback in the Buick, and she is happy, it is almost too much. She says, "Maurice, if people see us!" And he answers, "We are married, my wife, I'd like to see anyone dare!" And he kisses her again: maple sap, the sun's gold in their saliva. They are savouring their marriage which will be long, and long flourish, shameless forever. His two good hands gently press the palpitating blouse, and the pink breasts appear, swell, and then he becomes a little crazy and she lets him moan, sing his plenitude, exult, pressed against her from head to toe. The bride is in white and pink and the groom, bare chested, touches her, discovers her, desires her, seeks her. They both hear the sound of the sea, fear has disappeared, the sky stretches out forever overhead. Each kiss will now be free, death is outwitted, new life is begun.

Where did you find this picture that you are ever so gently laying on the pages? My heart skips a beat: they are there and I am with them, in Maurice's big row-boat, the very one that... I turn over the picture. Malvina's neat, beautiful handwriting, "Picnic excursion on Île de la Barque, July 1951." Maurice is sitting in the back, resting on the old, opened motor displaying its barbarous workings. My father has his beautiful Sunday-on-the-water face. Gertrude, my mother, is lifting her head towards the sky, you can see the amazed whiteness of her eyes. Her left hand is resting on Maurice's shoulder and the little gold ring shines on her finger, making a star-like mark on the picture. Malvina is sitting on the forward bench, her head turned towards us, absent-looking, as always, but I know her hands, fuzzy in the picture, are constantly twitching on her knees. Sam, meanwhile, is standing, his legs spread wide, one hand raised above his eyes, the other hugging the neck of a bottle concealed in a brown grocery bag. And I am standing on the wharf, in my swim suit, both arms stretched out to them, I want to get into the boat. It looks as though I'm about to fall, topple over. The sky is empty, immense above the wharf. No doubt someone asked a neighbour to take this picture that I have never seen.

I lift my head towards you, my love. I look at you, I smile, unable to speak. You know that it has just begun again in me, that acid purity of recollection, that fierceness of old suns of summers spent with them. That piercing, strident light of going off on picnics. You tell me, "I found it in a huge botanical book, in the attic. Was it a good idea or not to give it to you now?" I nod to you, and I take your hand. It is so hot that I shiver. You caress my hair, you say, "You already had beautiful legs, you know." I laugh, and you add, "If our own child was going to be as beautiful as the child you were, how happy I would be!" And then you go off in search of other treasures.

"Last night," thinks Big Gilles, "the barn owl's sad hooting went on a long time. It's a sign that a friend is coming. He is still far away but he's going to come, he's going to come." Gilles will tell me later, when I am ready, how he had seen, in his head, a little light come to life, move, kindling hope. "I don't know why nor how I see these things beforehand but I see them, that's how it is. Like I also know when the winter is going to be white and dry and when it will be wet and when the fields will stay bare. Like I knew that their church would burn and I told them so, but they didn't believe me. They say, 'crazy talk from that big crazy mountain man!' Too bad for them! They're sore at me in the village for this gift I didn't ask for and which makes them afraid. They prefer to whine and cry and keep these tragedies for a long time so they can talk about them in their kitchens and argue endlessly about what they call mysteries and about cruel fate. They do nothing. They wait. They await the next time someone drowns, or a steer disappears, or fire devours their barns. They can complain calmly afterwards, spend their winters moaning as they knit their mittens and scarves for the children and the dead. Talk about being blind! And they pay for masses and they rebuild the burnt-down houses and start over again, unendingly, stubborn like they are, indifferent to the law of the world. Inexhaustible in sorrows and desires. Never do they look, never do their eyes see the great life of the land, the depth, the clearness and the teachings, never do they stop to examine things, to penetrate their meaning. Always sticking their nose into bunches and bunches of misery, of bad luck, of wishes, of prayers, of rights, of privileges. Not one single look towards the river to know the waterfalls, the water's rhythm, its violence and peace, the lulls of time, the law that works for them and the thousands-of-years-old gold from the sun that gives us the round of the seasons, our own fortune. Never a blessed second of peace, always the hustle and bustle. I pity them. And then again, I don't pity them. In their stubbornness, everything is an excuse to condemn. They have forced me to disappear deep into the woods and poach. Because of their blindness and wickedness, others will be put aside, like me, and there will be much misery in the world. Because of their offices and their commissions, their sacraments and regulations, all their problems and so forth, I can't think about it, it's too terrible!"

In the twelfth trap, the one attached to the trunk of a big cedar at the edge of Rosaire La Tendresse's field (he's nicknamed "Rosaire the Harsh"), a little weasel is squirming. "They think I'm cruel. Yet they love to strut about in their beautiful fur coats on Sundays. Only, they wouldn't trap the animals, it's too dirty. They leave that to the big half-breed with the rotten heart, to the half-savage crackpot hillbilly! No, I don't like them, and it's eye for eye, tooth for tooth. I have peace instead of fear and indulgences. Come, little one, let's have some fun, let's make fun of them a little, both of us, eh?"

The weasel in turn goes into his bag. "Never again will I kill for their Sunday coats, on my word as big demon of the mountains! But I will have a full back yard of them the day they find me dead, frozen in my hut. Hares, weasels, fox, wild cats, white wolves and even a deer who will all jump them, they'll be so well-trained, eh Ti-fox? Because I know that too, that I will die one of these days, very tired of them and their aversion for life, set free from their contempt forever, eh, Ti-Fox?"

The fox has raised its head. A silhouette is motionless at the far end of the field. It's La Tendresse-the-Harsh taking aim. "Okay, let's go," says the Métis. Suddenly, he plunges into the bushes and disappears. The gun shot fades away into the mountain echo.

For the last few nights, I have been having the same dream: the boat leaves the wharf, the boat in the picture, and moves off into the night. Then I sit on the end of the wharf and wait. In my head, I hear, "They haven't gone very far." And then it's sunrise, and the boat does not return. I go back to the white house and look for you. You are not there. And in my head, then, I hear: "I knew it."

My love, I could bear losing you. It is not the solitude, nor the emptiness of the world, that would terrify me, were you to go away, to disappear. It would be the loss of something I had no longer been awaiting and which came to me like an undeserved present, like a radiant, breathless child running into a home in mourning. Do not be upset with me, my love, I am not used to glorious things lasting, to summers that keep their promises, to the dazzling consequences of mad love. You know how reticent I am about permanence, my fear of the great volatilization. The nightmare, my love, would be if childhood refused to open up, ceased glimmering, no longer allowed a world without death, an innocent world, ours. Then I could no longer be that limpid companion you deserve and need. I could no longer imagine what came next, we would smother. The child would not come.

You are sleeping. Do not listen to my voice, my love. Listen to the rain. The lake, this morning, is frothing the way it does before a storm, and the sky is black; gulls' cries fill the air. The storm will catch us full on in an hour. Sleep, my love, I shall take up the tale.

They swallow their soup. Each in her way. The first one, with the little spoon, most discreetly. The second with the big spoon, greedily, and she is wearing her bib like some delighted soul condemned to death. As for the third, she is hesitating because of the big, glowing eyes moving on the surface of her plate and the sad smell of cabbage which spoils her appetite.

On the little rostrum, at the lectern, Sister Angèle, applied, sonorous, purring, is reading: "There is joy in being a victim when it

is for Him..." She definitely said "Him", capital H, so that it will definitely be the Lord these sisters see in their imagination, and not the
other him, man and his savage selfishness. Between two delicate sips,
the first one takes the time, while blowing on her soup, to offer each
spoonful to her Creator and it is as though she was blowing on His
soul, assuaging his sacrifice, tenderly. The second one, between each
smooth sip, is battling the bad memory of the mean words her brother said, at the dinner table: "Fat pot of soup!" She hastens to swallow
the rest of her bowlful to dismiss the image of the big kitchen and of
the sly boy who martyrized her from dawn to dusk and she thinks,
alas, that he was quite right, that big brother: "I loved to eat and still
do, what a pity!" As for the third one, she is not thinking about anything, she is meditating again. All her attention goes to the white table
cloth, Sister Angèle's calm voice, and then nothing. A moving, fuzzy,
radiant fog captivates and bewitches her and then, blissful, she swallows the soup she does not like, has never liked, will never like, no
longer knowing its taste, nor even if it is still Sister Angèle who is reading the lives of the saints or simply a voice, any voice, in the limbo of
her mind which has fled into dream. It is only when Sister Angèle
rings the little bell that the third nun remembers, "Ah! Sister Angèle,
it was Sister Angèle and it was the life of Saint Catherine and it's that
cabbage soup that smells so bad!" What a pity to come back to earth,
especially to the big refectory where that sad odour of cabbage, odour
of penitence, odour of misery, floats neverending.

On the beach, shaded by a thick willow branch, Germain is sleeping
and Jacob is chasing away the mosquitoes prowling around his friend's
head. The wind makes little sun-scalloped shadows dance on the sand,
and on Germain's brown skin. It is noon, the big church bell is ringing
angelus. Once again, nothing's going to happen, thinks Jacob. He's
sleeping, the big cat. He's blissful, his nose in the air. How beautiful he
is! What would they think, in the village, if they knew I love him,
Germain? Not just the way you like a friend or a cousin or even a brother. I love him with my body; I can't help it. But I expect no deliverance

from this strange love. Nothing will ever happen."

Suddenly, Germain moves. His head rolls on the sand and he breathes strongly, his hair brushing Jacob's thigh, Jacob doesn't dare budge, for fear that... something will happen.

"You want to touch me, eh, Jacob? You've been holding it back so long, I've realized. You know, it's not sure I wouldn't like that..."

"That's it,", thinks Jacob, "he's the one sleeping and I'm the one dreaming!" Germain, of course, is the first to dare. His big, warm hand is on Jacob's knee as though to awaken him from his torpor, and calmly, the hand climbs the thigh, climbs, climbs...

It is noon and the sun is amused by so much innocence, this sin of tenderness beginning between the two cousins, on the little beach of Three Pine Bay. And which will not go very far, it will not have time.

Yes, it is noon. The world is full of light and I am like the cat, or like the little nun, the third one: I am seeking out the shade. I too need an oasis, amidst this ardent first day. I come down and join you on the beach. We both run to the big wharf to work up an appetite.

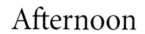

Afternoon

A big wind is pushing round, heavy, purple clouds over the lake. You are climbing the little slope on Malvina's old bicycle. Your hair is dancing around your head, your dress sculpts your body as though you had just come out of the water. I can see your teeth, you are smiling into the wind, the effort fills you with pleasure, you are radiant with challenge. I come down to greet you. You throw your arms around my neck and then, breathless, you say to me, "Ah, what a good wind!" We kiss, our mouths are like burns healing. I am holding the handlebars; you are walking beside me. Your dress billows, flapping like a flag. Once we are in front of the house, you tell me, "An Indian, on horseback, galloped beside me, he followed me to the foot of the hill and then rode off into the mountains. I've never seen such insolence, such beauty! He and his horse, in this wind, were..." You cannot find the words. Your eyes, however, are filled with the impetuosity that the Indian and his horse have injected you with, like a good poison.

You too, my love, are rediscovering something, renewing acquaintance with something, I know. For you also, exile, the white house, means childhood recovered, pure, intact, with its splendid violence of a newly steaming volcano. A little later, you bring me up this note that you quickly place on the pages:

Our child too will share that beauty and insolence. I want him to have that imagining memory you have, and now we have. I love you. Continue.

"Marcel, Reynald, Sylvia!"

She is calling them. She said their names gently, she did not shout. And then she remembered that her children were at school, of course, and that she was alone in the house. Alone, Rachel Bédard. And then, despite the smashing sunshine, it began: pain suddenly fell upon her shoulders, invaded the hollow of her back. A fever born from funereal images, from fear, from the great misery of these last few days. Everything was in order in the house, just a minute ago, and suddenly, normality is broken, the world has changed into a monster. Firstly, Léopold's rocking chair started to rock all on its own, and then the wind (and yet there is no wind) began to fill the curtains. Rachel turned her head so as to perceive her late husband's overcoat on the big hook, and yet she gave it to the poor yesterday, that thick overcoat smelling of the stables. Now it is starting to smell very strongly again, that overcoat, but not of the stables, no, nor of cows. The cloth is giving off fumes and fumes of wild scents, grassland perfumes, odours of pleasure, the suffocating emanations of the Indian and Léopold making love in the village woods. A cursed aroma of swamp and rot. Then Rachel Bédard feels very close to limbo, about to faint. Already she is staggering, she tries to catch hold of something, she is going to fall. She hangs onto the stove where a blinding reflection of the hot sun is flaming. "I've got to get outside, my God, or else I'll have an epileptic fit."

Outside, the stable comes at her like a reef that the boat, driven by the storm, cannot avoid. Its tin roof like hot coals, its incandescent walls, a real fire trap. Rachel opens the big barn door. The scent of hay does not calm her. On the contrary, it smells more and more of the sin of adultery, the cursed joy of love: Léopold and her, that Indian. "That woman who was taking him from me because she was giving herself shamelessly, legs wide open, on the grass carpet!" Rachel's head is spinning. "I don't want to become crazy, good Lord, do something, I can feel myself losing it, toppling into real madness, helpless, abandoned. Oh my God, my God!"

And then it suddenly stopped, as it had come. Because the little calf is there, the last born, hers, Chou-Chou, the one she pulled by the hoof and that came into the world in her arms. There he is, lying down, calm, and he is watching Rachel with his angelic eyes. Rachel knows then that she is temporarily free from the dragons of the dark tales, from the vision of Léopold and the *sauvagesse*. Chou-Chou sniffs at her skirt and

Rachel caresses him. Gentle, good, salty tears are flowing on her cheeks.

"Chou-Chou, my little guy, my little angel, my warm madness, my treasure, my little joy!"

The words come out, and it does Rachel Bédard a lot of good. So much, that she no longer thinks about being sick nor even about going mad. It's over. The big beam, the one Léopold hung himself from, is there, just above her. Rachel does not see it, thank goodness. There are moments of calm, of respite for those known as weeping widows: Chou-Chou's rough, warm tongue and his look of calm innocence.

The old Buick is raising a cloud of dust, a great, sparkling wedding veil, and the newlyweds, Gertrude and Maurice, my father and my mother, happy, are speeding towards the big white house, towards the other village, towards a difficult happiness, but one which will last. They are no longer afraid. Or rather, they feel only that fear you feel when the worst is past and the future opens before you, empty, dizzying. The fear of what can and must happen when nothing any longer prevents a love from soaring audaciously towards its uncertain future. The fear that remains after the struggle and the victory. The fear of not knowing, perhaps, what to do with sovereign time, what to do amidst endless happiness, what to do with new-found freedom. They look straight ahead: the fields, the road, the grey snake of the road, the surprising houses, the strangely-built barns, the new country. They think, once in a while, what it was like, not so long ago, to want each other so much and so much, and to be unable to even come close. They are happy, even with this fear of happiness, like two birds blown off their migration. They know they would die, both, together and immediately, if they came to be separated again. They will have the courage to face anything now, they know it.

Woodchuck whistlings, a few notes from an owl and, right by, at the very edge of night, the wind whistling in the poplars. I am kneeling in the middle of the bed, my head on your thighs. The window is open, the indigo night is trembling through the branches of the big pine. It smells good of earth and over-ripe peony. I glide my face towards your triangle, I inhale, drugging myself on your salt – a quick trip to the world's beginnings. You caress my hair as one pets the head of a child wanting to go too far into life's mysteries. The very precious secret of our joy is there, still shivering, deep within you. You who conserve, who safeguard, who prolong. You who will make the child. I move back up to your face. You smile, but your eyes are grave, your pupils dilated, you are dreaming. I dare not speak and break the enchantment. After a long while, you say: "I want her to know, do you understand? To know our love, the passion calling her, the beauty of this night. I want her to know the pleasure, the eagerness, the tenderness inviting her to join us here. I want her to know." I wipe away your tears of joy, your tears of doubt and drink them on my fingers. You hug me so hard that you leave me breathless. To lighten the atmosphere a little, I utter a little cry, like a trapped animal, to make you laugh. But even your laugh contains that violent, almost sad taste, that stubborn will that our child should know its origins, their wild gaiety, their deep gravity, their mystery like the beautiful disarray of our bodies on the bed, in the bright room.

Louis the barber, sitting on his doorstep, is meditating. No one in the shop, no customers, and Louis is calmly smoking. He is watching the fire of sun on lake. "All the gold in the world," Louis thinks. "When they say, 'I wouldn't want it for all the gold in the world,' (talking about some fancy that they're pretending not to want), they don't know what they're talking about. They're thinking about banks, gold coins, jewellery. They think about what they could amass in too short a life and which will never amount to much, anyway. Whereas true wealth, beauty, this frothing of molten sunshine, all the gold in the world, no one could give it. It is not ours. And yet, we enjoy it! We close our eyes a bit, and it comes to flame deep in the brain, it cleanses you like... Maybe that's it, the famous purifying fire. Ah, dear friends, the world, when you look at it right..." He is acting as though he were making a speech, Louis is. He is never alone, this barber. Somebody is listening, there is always someone who needs to know, to hear the words that celebrate, the words that cure vertigo. "Maybe I sound delirious, but just look at that: all the gold in the world, that's too much for a single pair of eyes! Let me tell you..."

Malvina has stretched out – oh, just for a wee moment! – on the bed she has so carefully prepared for the newlyweds. Fresh sheets of fine linen, a blanket of local wool, down pillows. The softness of the bed immediately swallows her up like a whirlpool. Could she have known? Should she have guessed that the skin of her back, on contact with the sheets, would start to burn, that she would start sobbing again, that the huge emptiness left by Sam would begin to shudder, to shake her so strongly?

She simply wanted to have a last nap in the bright room, simply breathe, in peace, eyes closed, to rest. "Now nothing will go as planned," she thinks. "May that not bring them bad luck, may my tears of sadness, all this mess, may it not spoil their wedding night, oh Lord!"

The mechanic's dog is sleeping now, head on his forepaws, muzzle in the grass. Now and then, he sighs deeply. Now and then, an ear suddenly palpitates. In the shade, by the water, he feels cool, he is in seventh heaven, he's resting, finally. A tiny taste of respite in the middle of a day that seems too enervating, sour, like the sap boiling deep within the stems.

Of course, Germain has gone to sleep. Sated, content, his big hand on his stomach, his breathing innocent, ample, all the air in the world in his breathing. As for Jacob, he is still chasing the flies, gnats, and dragonflies away from the too beautiful, too serene body of his cousin, the big cat. "It happened so fast, too fast and I was trembling like a little girl! Talk about too sweet a cataclysm! Frankly, I wouldn't have thought he would let me touch him like that. It was easy for him, of course. He didn't even open his eyes. And here I was thinking, 'The big cat is going to wake up, push away my hand, button up his pants, I can't believe this!'

Jacob's stunned eyes suddenly open wide. There, on Germain's neck, a mosquito is swelling redly, right before his eyes, with the big cat's scarlet blood. Troubled, infinitely troubled, Jacob observes the little vampire which, sated, tries to fly off. Ecstatic, heavy as death, the insect crash lands on the sand where it agonizes blissfully. "Me," Jacob thinks, "on the contrary, full of him, with his strength swallowed, with his blood, I could never ever die. I'd fly, I'd fly!" And Jacob shivers to have had so unreasonable and dizzying a thought.

Big Gilles runs into the clearing where his mare, Belle-Fille, is waiting for him, grazing on the bittersweet grass of the little marsh. With easy, natural gestures, he caresses the warm flank of the horse, ties the bag with the captive hare and weasel onto the saddle, then climbs on the horse without Ti-Fox stirring on his shoulder.

The rider, well settled in the dip of the mare's back, his hat pulled down over his eyes due to the bright sun, takes the mountain trail again. "I hope he's coming soon, this new friend. I'm like a bird with a broken wing. My heart is cold within me; I'm old. Today, if I saw him coming, I would forget all the wrong that has been done to me and die like an old man, satisfied and happy."

In the huge refectory, with its mother-of-pearl sheen, all three of them are moving quietly around the tables, delicately laying down bunches of trillium in small Sunday flower vases, for the priest's visit. The first one spreads out the lilies like a fan and knowingly seeks and finds the prettiest arrangement. The second one is making large clusters on the tablecloth, their violent red will catch the eye and perhaps suggest excessively alluring thoughts, come twilight. The third one is absent-mindedly, very absent-mindedly, weaving together stems, leaves, flowers and even some ferns and also, it just happens, two long stems of forsythia. And it just happens to be the most beautiful bouquet of them all.

Sam entered the inn with a bouncy walk and his hat on crooked. It will be his sixth whisky and a blissful haze has begun to numb his great sorrow, to postpone it until later. "I broke up!" he shouts to the waiter who watches him coming, shaking his head behind the bar.

"I broke up with her! To hell with the big white house and even more the far too good woman who was waiting for me, is waiting for me, will wait for me! A whisky, little guy, a big one! Also one for you if you feel like it. To the health of happy idiots, goddam Christ!"

Sam no longer knows where he is, where he's located, in what village, on which road, towards what impossible oblivion he is sailing.

Suddenly, I hear a growl, followed by strident little squeals. I leave the book, go open the window. You are in the water up to your thighs and, sun-drenched, you are looking at me. I shout, "Wait for me!" I undress going down the stairs and naked, I join you in the lake. The water leaves me breathless. You are jumping, shivering, beaming with joy. I laugh, and exaggerate all my movements to stop freezing. We fall together in an icy wave. We swim as far as the stand of bulrushes, you doing the breaststroke, me the crawl. Then we burst out of the water, running. The golden tint of your skin retains the bright drops longer. You come and stretch out on the chair saying, "He will like the cold water, too. He has to. It's so good!" I laugh. My love, I had lost that laugh a long time ago. That laugh of the first Antarctic swims, that childhood laugh, that laugh of the discovering body, I had forgotten.

Climbing back to the book, I imagine "She is here, she's moving, she's pulling the whole sky with her, she restores my desire to know, to be on the lookout, to spring up, to live!" I go back to the book where I left it, my shoulders washed and relaxed. All the beautiful spells of childhood are here again, with me, with us, my love.

At first, people thought they were tourists. Far too tender, exalted, immersed in their pleasure like story-book lovers, not caring how people looked at them, taking no interest in the people of this unknown village, nor in their mechanical comings and goings. Gertrude removed her wedding veil ages ago, and her hair is billowing, Medusa-like, in the wind. She has a supple, joyful stride. Maurice looks like one of those gangling heroes, hostile to reality, one of those cinema heroes, the sort they don't like out this way – because he is a real presence and because he is shamelessly in love with his wife, hugging her tight right in the middle of the road, kissing her against a telephone post. With that gaze he gives her, a gaze burning like hot coals in the wind. People dare not watch them too long for fear of knowing, understanding and being embarrassed. They would become aware of their narrowness, their sullen gestures, that's for sure, compared to that casualness of love that makes those two sway, hanging on to each other like drunks (folks will say: "like savages!"), and right in the middle of the road, openly and publicly.

They asked for some ice cream. She wants vanilla and he wants chocolate and "two scoops, please, Miss." The sun melts it on their fingers. They laugh and they lick the corner of each others' mouth (people will again say "like savages!"). People watch them out of the corner of their eyes. They are unaware that people are watching them like that, with such frowning attention. Who could possibly be interested in them, now that they are free? Now that they are walking together, touching each other, now that they are innocent? She in a white dress whose fine lace hem is dragging in the dust and who does not even give it a moment's notice and who is smiling at the sky, at her man, at the beauty of the world, without exaggerating, without making her teeth shine. He, meanwhile, is bare-chested, his shirt in his pocket, he tilts his head back and he laughs, devouring her with his eyes.

He takes her in his arms. She utters a light twitter like that of a bird being set free. He is carrying her. He walks clowning around with his beautiful, laughing load, right in the middle of the road. Around the old Buick, people, onlookers, the curious watch them kiss (folks will say, "eating each other, like savages!"). Then they set off again. The old Buick coughs, purrs, and finally decides to run smoothly. The bride suddenly bursts into laughter. Maurice has just made a splendid face at the curious people who were staring at them "like savages".

Rachel Bédard has plunged into her housework. "My God, my big spring cleaning not yet done." Wash the windows, the curtains, scrub the walls, sweat profusely, empty one's head of everything except a burning emptiness, a way of forgetting. Rachel washes, scrubs and scrubs so hard that a pane of the kitchen window breaks. A big blob of dark blood appears on her wrist. "My God," Rachel Bédard says out loud, "Fate bears a grudge against me. Blood, oh Lord, dark blood, that's all I needed!" She stays there, fascinated, watching her life slip by, as if at the end of the blood lay the peace she so desires.

"Mom, come on, what are you doing?"

It's Reynald, the eldest, come home early from school, by the grace of God, who finds her sprawled across the kitchen floor, covered in blood. Quickly Reynald rushes with a towel soaked in cold water. He stares at his mother. "She looks like a saint or a lunatic," he thinks. Rachel Bédard, saint or lunatic? Or quite simply a worn-out widow, a woman in deep mourning, betrayed, inconsolable, at wits' end. "We can't leave her alone any more from now on, that's for sure," Reynald thinks. He takes care of his mother, makes a tourniquet, stops the blood. The saint or the lunatic no longer notices anything, poor woman. "At any rate, I won't have to go to school, that's one good thing. We need a man in the house. Guess it's my turn. Starting today, I'll be running the household."

Rachel lifts her head towards her son. "How much you look like him, like your poor father, Reynald. I had never noticed." And she thinks, without saying it: "The same dreadful pride, the same curt tenderness, the same seemingly compelled love, the same grumpiness at having to care. It's sad, my God, it's so sad!"

Wakened, wrenched from his stupor by the torrid heat and the itching sensation of fleas, the mechanic's dog opens his eyes, gets to his feet, then stretches, bowing courteously to the beautiful weather, his snout in the sand and tail in the air. Then he scratches himself, his beating paw obsessed like the blade of a threshing machine. He shakes himself. In large, soft swells, his long body quivers, his ears flap and finally, of course, he loses his balance and finds himself sitting, nose against a mound of clay where a tantalizing odour makes him spring to alert, on the lookout, tail straight and ears squared. Slowly, his brain starts working again. At first comes a furry image, then gradually, as he goes on sniffing at the hole in the ground, it grows clearer. It has whiskers and moves like a shadow. It smells like the earth and musk, it's good, a little pungent, and wonderfully annoying between the fangs. A field mouse!

A big nervous quiver goes up and down his spine in little waves, reaches his paws, electrifying. Half appetite and half rage, that quiver. Suddenly, nerves tensed, hair standing on end, back arched into a camel's hump, the dog begins scratching the ground with his front paws. Mean, crazed, completely taken in by this new odour, lost once again, strung along by his muzzle, the poor thing. But the smell moves, it goes under a bed of old, dried-out branches. Then the dog jumps, swoops down on the odour that is already no longer there, has darted into the grass, an absurd, drifting little black dot. He falls on it with all his weight but the smell is already further on, fleeing. He thinks he's got it right between his paws! But the smell, the tiny black trail has escaped, has just returned home to its burrow. So the dog scratches, and scratches again, seeing red: he's hungry, poor thing.

The two innocent youngsters plunge into the forest along the big bay, a wood of pine and oak, unfamiliar to them both, which it is even forbidden to enter. That is written big as can be, in English: "No trespassing!" This forest belongs to the American hunters' club, property of Sir McDonald or Sir Maloney or some other rich Bostonian who bought it for peanuts, as you might expect, twenty years ago.

"'No trespassing', my eye, Jacob! The owners are far away, old buddy, in Boston or Florida or wherever. They only come in the fall to kill our deer, the bastards! Come on, I want to go see this."

Germain has jumped the fence in one leap. Jacob, however, hesitates. He looks at the lake, the sky, the row boat moored to the willow, he bites his lips, wrings his hands. Then he makes up his mind: he climbs the fence in his turn but the bottom of his pants gets snagged on a prickly barb. Germain burst out laughing, gets winded, coughs and finally says, "You're such a moron, my cousin!" The fabric in the pants rips with a disturbing noise and Jacob thinks, "I hope this isn't a bad sign. This better not be a bad sign!"

"Wait for me, Germain!"

"No trespassing!" It was written big as can be! And not only to forbid access to the American hunters' heaven. Because of the quicksand, the deadly sands of the English swamp, poor innocents!

The first one says, "Try again, sister, and louder for the love of God!" The second one adds, "You can do it, come on, don't go all tense like that!" But the third one blushes, then turns pale, swallowing her saliva, she could swear she was swallowing sand, and finally opens her mouth in a pouting smile. One, two, three, four. "O salutaris hostia..." That's better, much better even, and the other two voices rise to the rescue, crystal-clear, vibrant in the echo of the little chapel.

"O-o salutaris hostia..."

Corpus Christi, that's in just a few days, sisters, we must be ready, absolutely!

You call to me from the attic. I climb up fast, and find you in front of an open trunk with old rags coming out of it. You are wearing a blue dress with white polka dots, a little too big for you. You stare at me and, seeing my bewildered look, you immediately know: it is definitely Gertrude's dress, her maternity dress.

"I'm going to wear it, if that's all right with you. For good luck."

I look at you, speechless. The designs of fate make me shudder. It is not so much the dress, my love. It's that you look so much like her, and that suddenly time stands still, memory useless, useless the old pictures. Worse still: useless my efforts to recreate Gertrude, in the book. And then I realize you are stronger than everything, stronger even than memory. Beyond the life-giving words is life itself with its living flesh, its lighted attics, its surprises, its truth. There is you. I know that I have been the target of the game, from the beginning. Childhood surrounding me, seeking to deform me, to fold me, round me. It is assuredly the leader.

You say to me, "I bothered you, quick, go back down and work." You've got together, childhood and you, so that the words won't falter, so that they flow forth like streams.

"Malvina! Malvina!"

"I'm in the attic! Who is it, who's there?"

69

"It's me!"

"Who, 'me'?"

"Sylvia Bédard!"

"My gosh, wait, I'm coming down!"

Quickly, into the velvet-topped box, she thrusts pictures, letters, old, dry, crumbling corsages. Nimbly, she slips a picture between her skin and the material of her dress: Sam, arms wide open, hat in left hand, and with such a smile that his beautiful right hand, which he is stretching out toward her, Malvina, is all in itself a promise of paradise before the end of your days. My aunt comes down again from the attic and finds the little one, in tears, on the stairs.

"So what's going on, my child?"

"It's my mother...."

And then she starts crying, shuddering with huge hiccoughs of grief too huge for her. It looks like it is not just grief, but also a mystery.

"What, what about your mother?"

The child catches her breath, raises her head from her apron.

"If you saw her! You'd think she's lost her mind!"

"Poor child," thinks Vina, "if you only knew how fragile a mind can be." But she says nothing. The little one will learn well enough, on her own, and all in good time, the strange secret about being a woman, often neglected, tormented, alone. She will know it quite quickly enough. That exile can wait.

"Go, I'll follow you!"

Sylvia runs down the stairs. Malvina takes the time to adjust her blouse where the picture is held captive, her own pain, it may not drive her crazy, no, but which is better? To capsize with grief and topple over with it into oblivion, or to survive and suffer from a longed-for, impossible new start? "All the same," thinks Malvina, "poor Rachel, her husband hung himself cursing her, that's worse than anything, that is, that's hell on earth!" And now she is running, lifting up her skirts.

Big Gilles opens the cedar gate. The little deer hesitates. It taps its muzzle against the fence like someone very foolish or very shy. The half-breed has squatted down, he is waiting, his hand held out, open. The sunflower seeds make a delightful, appetizing noise between his fingers. So the animal beats its hoof against the ground, turns its delicate head from one side to the other, then slowly advances, ears drawn back, looking frightened. In the big half-breed's palm, a cool tongue, a warm nose, grassy breath, calmly insist. Then Gilles strokes the spotted, downy neck and the animal gives in, tamed, serene, rubbing up against him. "My helpless one, my beauty," big Gilles says, "you are the most beautiful thing under the sun. I have finished killing. I have stopped being afraid, stopped wanting vengeance. However, I haven't become useless. Not yet. A friend is coming, my beauty, perhaps I will be able to warm myself in rays of peace. I shouldn't have confidence in the future after having witnessed what happened and what did not. We are prisoners both, my beauty. But soon the gates of our isolation will burst. Roads wide as rivers cross the land, and along one of those roads, he's coming. I will teach him everything I know. After, I can die peacefully. The others will be able to play with the moon and stars, make war again, lose their way. But I shall pass away in peace."

The small deer leaps off. "Your hunger has eased, but mine, my hunger for giving, for sharing, my hunger for communicating, must still wait."

"But it's Samuel!"

"Where?"

"Over there, on the hotel steps!"

Gertrude, standing on the seat of the Buick, is vigorously waving her wedding veil. "Sam!" yells Maurice in his fog-horn voice.

"Sam, what are you doing here?"

"My God, he doesn't see us! Yoo, hoo! Sam!"

But the man has quickly turned his head, his hat pulled down over his eyes. There he is, grabbing the hotel barman by the neck and beginning to hold forth, arms in the air, yet without spilling a drop from his glass dangling at arm's length, it's truly acrobatic. Maurice runs and catches up with Sam just as he was about to fall, tumble down the stone steps, knock himself out maybe, or even worse, God knows what. The barman sneaks away, disappears into the hotel after saying to Maurice: "You handle it! I wash my hands of the whole business!"

Maurice has grabbed Sam by the shoulders, he's shaking him, pushing and pulling, talking loudly to him but Sam shakes his head again and again. He does not want to look at Maurice, nor listen to him. He continues his tirade to the wind, spinning like a weather vane, carried away like a tombola puppet.

"Do you know the story about the poor guy, a drunkard, who didn't want to enlist, who hid for two years in a barn, who almost went crazy, all alone in his barn, while the others crossed the ocean to kill or be killed? Eh? Do you know that story? Oops!..."

He fell anyway, despite the solid vice of Maurice's arms. But it was a soft fall, and there he was already starting to stand up again, or rather on all fours on the stairs, like a crazy dog, his nose in Gertrude's skirts.

"Sam, for the love of God!"

Gertrude picks him up and then he sees her, sees them both. In a flash, he completely sobers up, as if by miracle. Then he gets up and begins to run, staggering to his truck across the street.

"Sam, don't be crazy!"

But already the engine is running. Suddenly, the truck goes into reverse at full speed and bumps into the milk truck behind it.

"Sam, stop!"

The tires squeal, the truck roars off but too far to the right, so that the hood slams smack into the side of the milk horse which crumples, groaning. The truck has disappeared in a big cloud of dust. You can still hear it backfiring, further off, on the road south.

"My God, poor guy," says Gertrude. As for Maurice, he gives a big cough because of the dust before bending over the milk horse.

"We'll have to finish it off, poor thing."

There they are, both of them, faces and hands grey with sand, in the middle of the street, overwhelmed. A tornado just went through, stinking of cheap whisky, cousin Sam in all his fury. Where has he gone off, hell bent for leather? The sun, through the settling dust, throws a golden mist around the newly-weds. The horse is panting, its muzzle in the sand, moaning like a child. People have come out onto the doorstep of the hotel. They gesticulate, talk loud. Especially the milkman: it was his only horse. The man has raised his fist towards the road.

"A two hundred dollar horse, damn maniac!"

He has left only the tail of the field mouse, shiny and black, like the sloughed-off skin of a little grass snake. He is licking his chops, full. He had seemed berserk for a few minutes while he was deliciously crunching on the little beast, feeling the bones break between his teeth, against his gums. It was a moment of ecstasy, and now time is again reclaiming its substance, the landscape its place. Bitter excessive saliva is still exciting him, while all around the shapes drenched in blond light regain their power. So the mechanic's dog again finds himself alone, fateless, haphazard. Endlessly bouncing around among new smells, shadows, scents in the grass, trails in the sand that lead him on into abysses from which, out of breath, broken, he will surge forth, free and miserable. And then it starts again, a shadow, a fragrance in the grass... Hey, it's the cat, over there, stretched out on a rock, by the water, and oh so daintily licking the hair on its paws! Already the dog is getting worked up, he is going to leap without consenting to that hardening of his muscles, to that black celebration, to his racing blood. And there he goes, off like an arrow towards that rock by the water, lost, frantic yet again, fateless, haphazard, irresistibly propelled towards the cat, that obsessive red ball in the sunlight.

"Look Jacob! Over there, down in the ravine, a mother bear with her cubs."

"Oh yes, I see them."

Both of them, the innocents, have climbed high up an oak tree, Germain on the highest branch, Jacob a little lower, like two perched crows. The mother bear, glimpsed through the leaves, is a big black shiny mass that hardly moves, that licks her cubs from time to time as though to make sure that they are all there, richly odorous, intact. It is the first time Jacob and Germain have seen such a sight. They are spellbound, wide-eyed, jelly-kneed, hearts aflutter.

They could have climbed down the tree and gone their way, satisfied with that incredible vision. They could have resisted that desire, that crazy need to approach, that senseless desire to touch. But no. Germain, like a madman, clambers down the tree at full speed. He falls from such a height that he could have knocked himself out, but, barely groggy, he shakes himself, gets to his feet and waits for Jacob coming down, branch by branch, as if it were a ladder. Germain gets impatient.

"Hurry Jacob, for God's sake."

Hearing his cousin's shout, Jacob dropped, sure of landing on the softness of the sandy ground. Then they descend, the two innocents, clinging to each other, dazed, crazy, into the ravine.

It is raining. It is cold. The village, the shore and the white house are bathed in that grey light which makes day seem like an endless dawn. You have lit a fire in the fireplace. You are reading, motionless, curled up on this old cane sofa. The cedar logs release a pleasing, bitter smell. We hear the cries of seagulls circling the house. They are furious, those birds, when the weather is dull. I'm pretending to write, but, in fact, I've begun to sketch your portrait. Your profile is easy to draw. The pencil glides. Then, your long, curved eyelashes appear, your nose that always makes a little pout, your rebellious lock of hair, almost transparent on your round, sensuous cheek. You do not look much like yourself yet. I would like the child to inherit your proud, pure profile. Suddenly you have moved. Then the sketch becomes fixed, senseless, absurd. I smile at your motionless, untrue features on the paper. You get up, you go open the door for the dog who enters, groaning. He immediately comes to put his damp muzzle on my knees. You look at me, you smile, and then I realize about the book. I seize the immobility, the disloyalty of words and their deceitfulness. Like my sketch of you, the book is insufficient, misleading. Childhood is so vast, I will not even tell half of it. Today, I stop. I want to catch my breath for a bit, feel the white house in the present, and be with you.

I come close to you on the sofa. I watch you reading, I contemplate you, enjoy you, unreservedly. You turn a page, a piece of paper slides onto your knees. You pick it up. You read it, you smile and you hold it out to me. It's old, the beginning of a poem dating back to our time in town, before our exile. "It is sunny in the smell of sweat, and love suffocates under foreign concepts." You say, "That's beautiful, we should pin it somewhere." I get up with the poem. I go stick it on the wall, near the table, next to the photo, that famous one of the departure for a picnic. You come to look. You say, "That's right. That's where it belongs." You are right, my love: you are origin of the poem, source of the book, the picture come to life. You are the summer, all summers, past and future. You say, "I'm hungry. Aren't you?" Then I take you to the kitchen where the dog follows us. Breaking the bread, you say, "She's very near. I know it. I can feel it!"

Malvina is coming back from Rachel Bédard's. She has taken the little path that winds by the lake, bordered with blackberry thickets that are leafing out, little mauve spirals climbing along the thorns. The sun is at its strongest and the breeze, blowing from the lake, is loaded with odours. It smells of seaweed, sand and moss-covered stones. The water is still high, spring break-up was not so long ago. My aunt stops on the dam. "My God, how my heart is pounding, how it is pounding away! What's happening to me, though, is nothing, almost nothing. That poor Rachel, the sky's fallen on her head, her fragile head. She could go mad, it's dreadful! Whereas me ..." Malvina, suddenly you are out of breath. An uneasiness of no apparent origin, and perhaps without end, is buffeting you as you wind along this sandy little path. Your legs no longer obey you, they are stiff, locked up like cart wheels by a branch. Your two hands, like panic-stricken birds, rise up towards your scarf even though it is in its proper place on your head. You are trembling, Vina. You do not know it but you are shaking with shame and revolt. A storm in the hot sun. A rapid storm of the soul right in the heart of a magnificent day. A discreet earthquake. The continent is going to lose a rock, before long. A rock that will quickly become an island. You would not be any less surprised to see the church swept off into the sky or the lake open up its waters to swallow the road and the houses. You too are losing your mind. Or is it this bird whose frantic flight you were no longer expecting since you had clipped its wings, and which has started to flutter, to want to leave its cage of flesh, soar heavenwards? Is it then not dead, that crazy bird, from having struck and struck again against your heart?

Malvina looks at the lake, the sky, the treetops. She takes a deep breath; the bird quietens in its cage. "I had a narrow escape," she thinks, without understanding. "From now on, I'll have to be sensible. First, get through the summer, welcome the newly-weds, help them settle in, and be supportive to them. During the heat waves, avoid letting the body languish, keep working despite it all, forget. In the autumn and winter, it will be easier, the days are shorter. When Sam said goodbye to me, prancing on the steps of the veranda, I knew the seasons would be long. But I did not know all the rest. That distraction today, for example, my God, that distraction today!"

Malvina sets off again, her skirts in her hands, striding along as if not to be late reaching the big white empty house.

Rachel has gone to bed. You go to bed and you hope that this unhappiness will only be an illness, that it will fade away in the blood if you stay very quiet, very well-behaved in your sheets. Watched over by Sylvia who is making soup for her mother, the heat from Malvina's soothing hands still vibrant all over her back, her valerian drops on the night table, Rachel Bédard is waiting. She tries to believe it is a physical illness, fatigue. "The doctor is going to come, everything will be all right. The body is a temple of wisdom, all you have to do is exorcise it, and then the nerves, the veins will once again connect to the main line – you're reborn. If I could sleep, just sleep! If I could, by closing my eyes, stop seeing those two, lying in the meadow, stop hearing their diabolical laughter!"

She has closed her eyes. This time, it is pure magic:

Rachel just dives, dizzyingly, she takes a great leap into nothingness. Everything dissolves around her, her mind empties: Rachel Bédard, is, finally, going to sleep.

With Uncle Sam's binoculars that you found while rummaging through the big trunk in the attic, we observe the birds on the shore. This morning, there is the plover who runs as fast as he flies and who pecks at thin air, like a mechanism gone awry. A big heron, meanwhile, does not budge. Anchored some way out from shore, it is keeping watch for its prey, no doubt a small silvery carp which the sun will give away. Two teals zigzag along, you would think they were dancing on the water. Their sky-blue flight makes you utter an enchanted, cooing "Oh!" Suddenly you scrutinize the empty sky, you sweep the horizon, and, pointed at the mountains, the binoculars come to a standstill. With your free hand you touch me and you say, "What is this?" I come to put my eyes where yours were. The mountain is shimmering in the halo of the lenses. I steady your hand and I immediately see, as if it were coming towards me, the fairy's cave. I give you back the binoculars and, while you stare at the cave entrance, I explain to you. I went down it once, with Big Gilles. The Métis had told me, "Down there, it's the centre of the earth. You go down, you spend a whole day in the earth and when you come back up you are cleansed of age, of time, of rot." You say, "Is that true?" I do not know. I only remember what I said to Big Gilles once I had resurfaced into the light: "I have a soul! I can feel that I have a soul! A soul at one with my body, not a catechism soul!" He responded then, "It is the soul of the earth that gave it to you." You say: "That's all? But that's astounding!" You look at me with your explorer's eyes. I do not know how to make you understand. They were so simple, all those sensations revealed by the Métis. My childhood is full of them. It is only with time that they became weird, inexplicable. I did not imagine, then, no more than Big Gilles, that one day I would catch myself being astonished by my memories, that one day I too would become unfathomable, a prisoner of magic spells. You press me with questions.

You want to know what it was like underground, what I saw, if it was dark, if it was cold. I say, "You feel smothered, at first, you struggle against an obtuse fear. Fear of insects, fear of roots, probably the fear of death. And then, after a while, you feel invulnerable, strengthened by the rock's eternity, you are sure that nothing ever again will scare you." You stare at me as if you no longer know me. Alas, I am used to that stare. For a long time, it hurt me. In school, every time I began to recount my adventures with Big Gilles, going on and on, obsessed, I would earn myself tilted heads, unbelieving eyes, sometimes even obvious contempt. But your look is kindly, bolder, more adventurous. So I talk to you at length about that day, about my trip to the bottom of the fairy's cave. One by one, my body rediscovers the emotions, the bewitchment, that sort of vibrant awakening of the cells, the frightening dizziness of discovering that one is oneself an abyss, a gulf, of knowing one is mortal and at the same time eternal, of knowing one is alive. And then, all of a sudden, one knows. One knows that everything goes on living, that the dead are roots, that the soul has found refuge in the clay, that it awaits, that it lives, still and forever. You know you are simply blinded, that the spirits are endlessly speaking to you, wanting to touch you, you know there is no stopping, no death, that you cannot decide anything because it itself decides, that the earth is round like a ball, that it will never let you go, that there is no elsewhere. You know that it is better to be like the animals and stay confident, develop your kinship with the world, it is the only way. Do not separate yourself from life's forces, accept the earth's motherhood, you know that such is salvation.

I stop, breathless. I realize that my impassioned speech has made you grave, solemn. You nod your head but I know you are very serious when you say, "I want to go down there. I want the child also to know. I want him also to be born confident, protected." You train the binoculars on the mountain again and glimpse a peregrine falcon soaring over the pines.

Of course, they followed Sam. The Buick turned onto a dirt road, behind the truck. Slowly, however, because of the dust. Often they have

78

to stop, wait for the blinding cloud on the road to settle. Fortunately, they can hear the truck. They advance, so to speak, by ear. Gertrude is worried. Her face has gone pale, dusty with sand.

"But where's he going like that, you want to tell me?"

"I don't know. Unless he wants to..."

"To what?"

"Nothing, nothing."

Maurice dares not say what he dreads. The dust has settled, the Buick starts off again, forging ahead in pursuit of the truck in an unknown countryside which seems hostile, given the circumstances. They do not have to go very far. The truck is there, all of a sudden, half-way into a ditch, at a sharp bend in the road. The Buick stops. And the newly-weds get out to see. Nothing, nor anyone. One of the truck's wheels is still turning in the air, as if moved by the devil's breath.

"There, in the field!"

Once again, Gertrude spots him first. Sam is running, trying to run, he is prancing in the middle of the field, sinking into the muddy furrows. You would think he wants to head for that barn at the end of the field, a sort of old, dilapidated shelter with holes all over.

"Come!"

Their wedding day, scarcely ordinary already, finds them climbing a cow fence, chasing after a poor devil at the end of his tether and his moonshine.

"But where is he going, for the love of God?"

It will not be easy to stop Sam, to reason with him, to take him back to the white house. "And anyway," Gertrude will tell me later, when my unending curiosity will get her all steamed up, "with a man under the influence, you can't do what you want, they're capable of the worst!"

Sam laboriously made it into the old barn. They stay there, the newly-weds, right in the middle of the field, mud up to their calves. After a while, they hear a dreadful moaning. They begin to run towards the barn, sinking into the ploughed field.

That afternoon, in front of the post office, in the car, I told you about the shopkeeper, the one who had brought me back to the white house after the first time I ran away. And then we went in to get the mail. The shopkeeper was there, aged, grimacing, a parcel in his hand. He greeted us, I was pale with astonishment. He looked at us a long time, then he said to you, "Excuse my bluntness, Madam, but I thought I was having visions. It is as if I was seeing his father and mother again. You both have that same pride and that same spontaneous look. Excuse me again." Then he left. You looked at me. I believe I smiled, but I was finding it a bit too much. No, not too much. Upsetting, frightening, oppressing. You embraced me, and said "It's the book, it's normal, everything happens."

I do not know why, but the sun leaped at my face as I was leaving the post office. The sun or else a very ancient ember, still unknown and which was rising from very deep, like a surge of fever. But come to think of it: didn't the old man look at your stomach? But of course, his eyes were staring at your stomach. I am certain of it. That flush on the face, that's what it was. It is the child who is visible on you, on your skin. It's the child coming.

As for the resemblance, of course, the store keeper is right. But that, we knew already.

All three of them are walking in the convent courtyard. The first facing the second and third. They come and go, forwards and backwards. You would think they were two small, unequal battalions, aligned for a combat that just cannot get started. And they're talking, how they are talking! You cannot hear what they are saying because of the cries of the little girls playing hit ball in the courtyard. From time to time, a dishevelled, red-cheeked little girl walks up to the first or the second or again the third to say, "Excuse me, Mother, but you're walking on the game." Then the first shrugs her shoulders, smiling, too certain of her unchangeable path to stoop so low as to make the effort to move over, tough luck for the ball game. As for the second, she opens her eyes wide, looks at the young girl and says "But, young lady, you have the whole yard!" And she spreads her arms wide to show the space, all the space that there is over there to play in. The third, well, she laughs, her hand in front of her mouth, thoroughly amused to see the little girl pushing, pulling on the skirts of the little Sisters. And in fact, the child is right. Playgrounds are made for playing, it's sacred, recess is sacred!

Frantically taking to their heels, the two innocents hurtle down the slope of the ravine. The mother bear is bellowing behind them, striking down old branches and spruce in her rush, with a great, furious noise. Quickly, Jacob climbs up a tree, scraping the skin off his stomach and knees. Germain, meanwhile, is still running madly towards the marsh. The she-bear passes by (Jacob holds his breath in the tree) then she slips, falls and tumbles down the large crevice, bellowing a ferocious cry that echoes against the walls of the ravine. Then suddenly, the woods fall desperately silent. Only the leaves are shuddering on the tree a trembling Jacob is perched in. After what seems to him to be an eternity and without having caught his breath, Jacob screams, "Germain, are you still alive?" And it is the echoes that respond, "Are you still alive ... alive, live..." Crazed with distress, Jacob has closed his eyes and, strengthless, lets himself drop. A sharp pain in his knee wakes him up, "No, no, not that! Mercy, not that!"

By dint of meandering, aimlessly, exhausted from swimming, feeling panic rising in him, his numb front paws flopping, the mechanic's dog is beating a whining retreat. The moment his back paws touch bottom, he lets go, plunging his head under water, his snout sinking like a rock. Then he bursts up, suffocated, and washes up onto the beach, half dead. From there, he still can glimpse the red cat, all its hair in the wind, seated very nonchalantly on the bow of the boat heading out. The fisherman, who happens to be Aldéric Guindon, did not see it jump in the boat. Cleverly, the cat hid under some canvas, patient, sure it would quickly get a chance to enjoy a nice, greasy little perch just as soon as Aldéric turns his back.

The dog has no more breath, no more rage, no anything. He stares at the boat without any emotion. He watches the reddish flash disappear, plunging into the bottom of the boat. The dog cannot remember what he had found so fascinating, just a while ago, in this insane cat, this poor beast as lonely as he. It will only be when I become his friend that he will stop being alone and frightened, that mechanic's dog. That will be the end of the hapless, meaningless part of his life. Then he will know that he lost nothing by waiting. Nor did I.

Without anyone sensing it coming, the wind has started to blow, to move large clouds going so fast they seem joyful, curling up then unrolling like balls of wool falling from a gigantic spinning wheel. These are storm clouds, still harmless, making great moving shadows on the fields. It must be four o'clock in the afternoon, judging by the slanting shadows of the trees bordering the township. If you listen closely, you can let yourself be charmed by beautiful music the south wind makes with the pine needles, a wind said to be nasty. It sings tunelessly, and, if you try too hard to hear it, that little music stops, and you have nothing but the wind in your ears. I hear it. It upsets my breathing, that music does, it ... But I'm trying to go too fast. It's because this singing wind mocks me deep in my nothingness. Let's say that it wakes me early, to give me a hint. Well do I know, if I follow it, where it will take me. Already, we are passing over the white house, the wind and I. The little music has fallen silent. Suddenly I start whirling, the wind plays with me and it is as a little whirlwind that I force open the window of the bright room, that I make the curtains fly, that I fall on the bed, dazed. The bed. Its beautiful oak posts, sculpted with wide open vine leaves whose veins take the light and lead it to the beautiful embroidered pillows. And it is there that I will come to them, at first in a breath, like the little music. And after, they will fully invent me, taking their time.

The wind makes the window bang and here I am returned to my limbo, to languish. I am going to miss this storm. Too bad. There will be others, even more beautiful.

Rachel Bédard is dreaming. Motionless in her bed, beneath two bedspreads, and yet she is standing in the middle of the meadow with Léopold's savage staring at her like a spectre. "Go away," shouts Rachel, "go away, damned witch." But the savage does not go away. On the contrary, she starts undressing, the skins slipping one by one into the grass, revealing her black body, her ebony flesh, her witch's nakedness. "Your teeth, your cursed shiny teeth!" The Indian pays no attention to Rachel's words, despite her screamed insults. She smiles, showing them, those bright teeth. She is beautiful, dangerously beautiful. Now she is lying down in the grass, her skin and the leaves make a beautiful, silky, then ripping sound, releasing the intoxicating scent of her woman-for-any-man sweat, the sweat of a free woman born for cursed love. The Indian has opened her legs. All the brilliance of the sun takes refuge between her flaming thighs. Her genitals are hot coals burning red in the middle, they are calling, they are hell, they are going to consume Léopold who approaches her, panting like a crazed animal. "No," cries Rachel, "don't go! She wants your death, that savage! She's the devil, Léopold, the devil!" Rachel's shout has made the Indian, Léopold, and the fire in the grass all flee. Only the wind remains, alone, in the pasture, and also that round spot where the grass was flattened by their now absent bodies. But she'll be back, that Indian, Rachel knows it for sure. A witch is a witch, that cannot be helped. Neither scapular nor holy branch can change that. Yes, she'll return, with her glistening skin, her too-white teeth and her poisonous scent, that savage.

You are on the gallery, you are looking through the biggest window, one hand over your eyes. From the path, I shout to you: "Come, there's nothing to see!" But you do not budge. You seem to have spotted something in the Bédard house, the haunted house, as the villagers call it. Suddenly you shout, "Come and see!" Your voice is worried. I sigh, and then I go up to join you on the gallery. I look. An old mould-spotted velvet sofa, a table covered with plaster debris. On the wall, a calendar showing Jesus revealing his radiant heart. That is all. The room is bathed in light that seems amber with age. You say, "Have you seen the year on the calendar?" I look again. The boards of the old gallery creak underfoot. I can see 1957 right at the top of the calendar. The semi-circle of finely-wrought digits hugs the shape of the halo over an entranced Jesus. I say to you, "They left the house, that year." You seem oppressed, it seems as though you want to unburden yourself of something. Without thinking, you say, "Were you born?" I answer, to make you laugh, "No. I was born two years ago, one winter, when I met you." But you do not laugh. So I say, "I was ten when they left." You look at me, troubled. You come back down the stairs, you stop at the little gate that groans open as your hand pushes it. I rejoin you, and ask you what's wrong. You say nothing's wrong. That it just gave you a funny feeling to see that old calendar, that intact, belated, haunting date. You sit down on the ground, take a deep breath, and start speaking. You say that the room, that sad museum, that calendar of arrested time have awakened some ancient morbidness. You confide to me an old fear, a recurrent childhood fear, a nightmare vision.

"When I was running a fever, I used to watch the objects in my room: the knickknacks, a blessed branch over the door, the calendar, my toys. I would say to myself, 'Those things are eternal, they'll outlive me. I am going to die, and those fantastical, immortal objects will remain.' Then, those objects would start to dance, a swirling snake-dance in the bedroom from which I, already, had disappeared. I had fallen to the bottom of the abyss, vanished!"

You stop, breathless, pale. Then you look at me, and say, "This house, I shouldn't have. You see, I too can sometimes be unhealthily curious." I laugh, and say: "You too?" It's your turn to laugh, you breathe deeply. The little gate squeaks as I close it. We walk towards the beach. I am quite aware, my love, that I am not the only one to be irresistibly drawn, sometimes, by haunted landscapes. Childhood, inextricably, mixes life and death, the ephemeral and the eternal, sad bedrooms and marvellous gardens. I think, but do not say to you: "He too will be haunted. We all are. All woven from the very fibres of a time and space inhabited prior to us and after us, all imaginative, all visionaries. We are all mortal."

You kiss me and send me back to the book, and you go run on the beach, set free. It is that suddenness, that tranquil wildness, that haste for pleasure that, in you, haunts me now and forever.

The sky has clouded over. Already, to the south, shrouds of rain, iridescent with sunlight at the bottom, are falling slantingly onto unknown fields. Lightning is piercing the clouds which, still silently, come sliding over the roof of the run-down old barn, like distress signals. Gertrude and Maurice, trembling, have entered and are holding each other in a motionless embrace on the step of the big door that creaked. Over there, in the hay, beneath the vault of beams, a strange world lights up, taking shape as their eyes become used to the dim light in the barn. First they notice a bed, right on the straw, with blankets and also an eiderdown that Gertrude recognizes since she is the one who had sent it to Sam for Christmas five years ago. At the foot of the bed, a circle of burned stones, a kind of fireplace covered with an asbestos plate, holed to let out the smoke, and a pipe twisting towards the tattered roof. And then, all sorts of tin cans on some kind of shelf fixed to the wall. And over there in the back, massive, shining, monstrous: the still. A big barrel with rubber tubing and tin spokes, next to a little farm machine motor. My father and mother look at each other, stunned: "But, but...,"Gertrude murmurs. Maurice does not say a word. He slowly approaches, and he is the one who discovers Sam, stretched out in the hay, snoring, his right hand clasping the neck of an empty bottle. Gertrude has approached too. "Dear Lord, I can't believe it," she says. Maurice gazes all around and rummages up a jar of instant coffee.
"Make a fire, my love, we're going to wake him up."
Gertrude hoists her bridal gown again, now her poor, torn, mud-spattered gown. She piles planks in the fireplace, grabs the damp matches and kneels to find twigs. Outside, it's pouring rain. "God, what a day!" says Gertrude. "I love you, my wife!" shouts Maurice who for a moment stops shaking poor Sam to smile at his bride.
All three of them are kneeling and the little girls with them,

crammed into the tiny convent chapel. They are praying. Their voices are trembling, frightened.

"Dear Jesus, protect our convent!"

"Dear Jesus, protect Daddy, Mummy!"

Then the first clap of thunder hammers down just as a lightning bolt shatters the tree that bursts into flame and crumbles, half of it in the playground. The first one says, "Thank you, Dear Lord!" and gets up to light the candles. The second one sighs loudly, staring at the charred tree. She says nothing, she is still too afraid. The third has fainted and the little girls are bustling about her: "Sister, Sister, you're alive, it hit a tree, just the tree, Sister!"

Big Gilles is standing, arms akimbo, head raised to the sky. He is naked, magnificent in the lightning flashes. Later, during a similar storm, he will tell me, "Take off your clothes, stand naked under the rain and you'll see: nothing foreign, nothing stubborn will remain in you!" And he will smile dizzyingly, his wild pupils dilated like a screech owl's.

Malvina has shut the window of the bright room, she lets herself fall on the bed. She ran up the stairs so fast! Now, the rain will beat in vain, hurtle down with all its strength and with thunder and lightning on the white house, unleash its force to its heart's content, the bedroom is protected, vaccinated. My aunt is not afraid of the storm. There she is, climbing back up the stairs, climbing the ladder, returning to her pictures, the photos of Sam to protect him too from the storm. "Samuel, my big fool, nothing must happen to you!"

She used to say: "Everything discourages me. Ever since your mother and father left, and then you, I haven't got the energy to do anything, if only you knew! All I've got left is this house, with its beautiful memories, its terrible memories too. I'm leaving it to you. Turn it into something cheerful, you still can." Her hand would tremble on the sheet. My aunt was going to die, taking with her her great dream of health, beauty and grace. She was bequeathing to me the future, light, luck: the white house. The downstairs bedroom, the one overlooking the yard, her death-bed room, Vina begged me to shut it forever. She used to say, "Leave my room as it is, shut the door, that's all. When you pass in front of it, think of me, that will do me good. As for all the other rooms, let the light in to wash away the past. I beg you, my nephew, live, you do so deserve it!"

That was last November. I went for short walks on the beach. I had lost everything, I was recovering everything, but too late. Black moss had appeared on the stones. The air smelled of marigold, muck, the end of life. The wind was blowing so hard it seemed to me the mad wind would carry away the beach, the white house, my fragile aunt, the boat, the wharf before I had even recognized them. I sometimes wished that wind would carry everything away, that a tornado would burst forth wreaking havoc, annihilating the village. I wanted anything, horror, a cataclysm, anything except this slow, unfair death in the dark room. I hated myself to death for having been away so long, for no longer being able to do a thing. I went back in to see her. It seemed as though she had got even thinner in an hour, in ten minutes, that you could see her getting ever gaunter, minute by minute. Her eyes stayed closed, her pupils were vibrating, her immobile, half-open lips released a death rattle, a remnant of breath. The doctor had said, "I can't do anything, she simply doesn't want to go on."

Then, shrugging, he left, with his heavy footfall of the living on the stairs. She died that morning. I opened the window. The breeze blew upon the lace, the dried flowers, raising a dust of times long gone, the crumbling of her unlucky star.

You came with me to the cemetery. Since I had met you, death had lost its grip on me. But I was tired, empty. You remember, you stopped me from striking the new priest who had started to speak of life everlasting, of rest, of blessed bliss. On returning to the white house, I closed the door to her room, as she had asked. We had never gone inside until this morning.

You precede me into the dark, camphor-scented room. You do as I did: you open the window. But this time, sunlight floods in, the wind billows in the curtains. A wind that smells of sand and water. I join you near the window. Together, we look at the bed, the spruce wardrobe, keeper of my aunt's treasures, her pictures, her letters, her drawings I knew nothing about. Trees. Nothing but trees, twisted or straight, immense, mostly poplars. We look at everything, exhume all. Today we are exorcised, forgiven profaners. Finally, you even say, "This will be her room." I do not stir. Of course, you are right. That is what Vina wanted when she said, "Turn this house into something cheerful."

You lie down on the bed. I come close to you. You take off your dress. Your beautiful arms, above your head, like the gesture of a priestess. The wind blows on us, free, escaped. Malvina is happy, I am sure of it. Happy that we are like that, passionate, magnificently determined to make the child in her home, on her bed, and with this good wind blowing in through the window and drying our sweat as it comes. I close my eyes while I move with you and I find myself again in the cascade where, as a child, I used to go so often, alone, the cascade in the little river with all the turtles. And it is, today, with you, as it was in the middle of the current. By holding my hands in front of me, I make the burning water diverge, cascade. My motions guide the water, shooting it onto my back, my thighs, my belly. Will she know, our child, that she was, first of all, this fish going upstream, this rapid shiver of pure silver beneath the surface of the river, its mother, you?

The mechanic's dog is caught by the storm, standing on the beach, head slanted, mouth completely crooked, his fur beaten down smooth by the rain. He is so alone, so distraught in the gigantic downpour. Suddenly, he looks towards the white house. Is he beginning to guess that I am coming along into the world, that the storms will no longer be furious like this one, ever? That the rain will no longer be demented? That fate's bad knocks will no longer take from him his desire to run, to lift his muzzle for anonymous caresses so quick to change into kicks, sharp pains? I will tame him, indeed, the mechanic's dog. It will take some time and he will come to feel some measure of happiness, but will he be able to let himself go completely, as his animal soul made for man, and more surely still for the child of man, has already wanted to? Too much a loner and too suspicious, for too long mistreated by life, he will let himself be patted, he will obey, he will bring back the stick, but there will always be, in his eyes, some torment that will make me love him more than all the comfortable dogs yet to come, after him.

Louis is going to close up shop. He's going to make his way with the other men to the nuns' convent, to bring help. "That was a fine clap of thunder," Louis thinks, "it cracked like a shot from a German, Japanese or French canon. The war must have been like that: a continuous storm, the sky thundering, men ablaze like torches, like the convent tree. I would never have made it back from the war, that's for sure!" And he smiles, Louis does. His fine moustache, his Hitlerian mustache above his thin lips, like Tino Rossi's.

He puts on his rain hat and takes off running. Just when he crosses the main street, a phosphorescent flash of lightning, a real ball of fire makes the black sky tremble above him. Louis stops, curls up, waits for the clap of thunder that doesn't come. As he gets up, he thinks, "I would for sure have stayed there, on the battlefield, there's no doubt about it. Dead or crazy, but I would have stayed there!"

Jacob is scared to death. He is shivering, seated under an oak tree, his smashed knee between his hands.

"Germain, big cat, where are you?"

The echo from the ravine no longer answers him. The thunder is already rumbling more to the south, and the sky is slowly tearing open to the west. A ray of sunshine passes through the misty undergrowth and reaches him. Then Jacob gets up, on that little note of hope. He hardly feels the pain in his leg any more. Holding on to the low branches, Jacob undertakes the climb down to the bottom of the ravine. "He's got to be alive, he's got to." But he's already getting worked up. His clumsy, frantic hand catches a dead branch that breaks and Jacob falls, rolling head over heels, hurtling down the slope of the crevice. For a second, he has another bout of pain, sharp, unbearable, and he falls back into limbo, wet emptiness, the floor of the ravine. Before completely losing conscious-ness, he has time to glimpse, hazy, unreal, the English marsh.

"We all," Maurice, my father, will tell me later, "believe we each live our own lives with their ups then their dizzying downs. But no! Like it or not, we're like ants in their hole: a single fate, just one, to share, like holy bread!" He will be solemn and pompous, that Maurice, from time to time. But he will be right, of course.

I, at this point in time, am still in limbo. Limbo! This is what they say in the village in order to try to name this space and time before life, where I am. Small, still empty egg cuddling in Gertrude's belly, I am waiting. I await my father's love, his lightning flash, fertilization, as they call it. Limbo – that's also the afterwards of life, when you die too early, in other words without being baptized. And sometimes, something similar, when you lose consciousness, a sort of coma, if you will. It says so in the little catechism, it is holy writ. But for me, it's already a flesh-red, innocent sky, well before skin and organs. Everything is flesh even before being flesh, that's how it is. Limbo is this big eye of blood through which I see every-thing, infinitely attentive, living. I'm preparing myself to have bones, nerves, dreams, thought, skin, densely woven skin, shivering skin, my mother's skin, a heart for joys and pains. At first, my head will be bigger than my heart, but that will not last. My heart will grow. Yes, at first I will be this small, fragile tadpole, this big spiralling brain, swimming in a lake of blood that will nourish me, motionless because too fast. I am already begun, soon I will be this tiny, slightly weird frog, this small opening bud, this traveller of blood and light.

My love, the bright bedroom is ready. It is awaiting me. Awaiting the child. The window is open wide to the storm-washed sky. It's late afternoon, your favourite time. Come. The book will wait. I shall go back to it later. At twilight, I shall return to it.

ROBERT LALONDE

Twilight

Maurice's old canoe is there in the shed, his bark canoe made by Lewis Roussin, an Iroquois from the cove. The boat is in very fine shape, light, the two of us carry it quickly on our shoulders all the way to the lake. You paddle at the bow, I at the stern. I try to remember the gestures, the flexibility, the balanced swings. The palm of my hand adapts well, my left arm stretches out easily, my right arm plunges. We are gliding smoothly ahead. You tie up your hair, the breeze is strong. A large cloud hides the sun that is warm nonetheless. We glide towards the big bay. Your head turns from side to side, you follow the silky path of the water lilies on each side of the canoe. The bulrushes brush against us, hissing like snakes. Barely breaking the surface, small silvery carps zigzag, terrified by the shadow of the paddles. A water serpent threads its way along my paddle blade, stops, and fixes its big, threatening eyes upon me, sparkling like zinnia buds. We disturb two plovers who whirl around us, screeching so as to distance us from their nest. The white sand of the bay is like a slice of sun set on the blue-black slice of waves. You turn around, smile at me, your paddle raised like a standard. I raise mine; we salute each other, motionless. Then we drift a little. You let your hand drift in the water, you gather a little in the hollow of your hand and throw it in the air: diamonds that dance between the sun and you and come down as unpolished pearls, piercing the surface of the black water. I plunge the paddle to touch the bottom. We are nearing the treasure. About two hundred feet from the shore, between the large willow and the stand of blackberry bush, I leap into the water screaming like a movie Apache. You get splashed; you shake your head, still holding the paddle in the air. I come to grab the bow of the canoe and I hold it until my torso emerges from the water. Then I dive. In less than ten strokes, there it is, it has not moved, just a little more covered with algae, full of sand and oysters – the church bell. I soar up like an arrow. You watch me as if I were a drowning victim come back. I say to you: "Dive, I'll hold the canoe." You arch upwards, then there's that beautiful bend I envy: you dive in smoothly, without a splash. Then it's my turn to dive. I take your hand, we swim all the way to the wreck. Underwater, your eyes are larger, more astonished. You resurface to take a deep breath and then you dive again. You come and touch, caress the ooze of algae around the large rusted bronze clapper. You look at me through our bubbles. We resurface. Gripping the canoe, we pant for breath. Gasping for air you say, "Explain that for me. That bell, what's it doing there?" I explain, without taking time to catch my breath, "When the church burned, two Iroquois, in fact the two arsonists, stole the bell and went to swamp it off the end of the wharf. The bell travelled with the current, it became embedded in the sand, right here. Do you realize? It had come from Rome, that there bell." You're laughing so hard I don't know if you believe me. I help you get back into the canoe. Evening arrives, we paddle towards the white house. From time to time, you turn around and then I receive your hearty laughter right in my face.

As we disembark, your eyes are still mocking me and you tell me, "I hope that our child will be as wonderfully crazy as you." I am a little miffed, so I tell you, "But that was true about the bell. The day I found it, Sam told me the story. It's true!" You say, "I believe you, I believe you!" And you laugh even more. I'm not the prankster, my love. It's the village. It's the past. I had forgotten everything: the church bell, the canoe, the strong current, the water snakes, the white house, all the childhood allegories. Suddenly, now, I want to recognize everything, to reinvent everything, to ride the magic carpet until the end. I say, "After the child, I will know how to become normal again, don't worry!" You are not smiling when you answer, "Why? That would be silly, you're happy like that, so stay like that."

It's true: with this new memory, accurate, inventive, haunted, I rediscover well-being, a certain grace, an easiness that had become extremely rare. Nevertheless, the curiosity to learn everything again, this resurrection, I owe to you.

The first is lighting the candles and the Chinese lanterns, the second is deeply inhaling the odour of melting wax, a sensual yet holy odour. As for the third, she is kneeling – you can hear her knees crack – before the Virgin and her outstretched arms.

"Ave Maria, gratia plena..."

The rest of the prayer is mumbled because the third's tongue is sticky with the saliva of beatitude. Between her and the radiant Virgin: sudden, perfect tenderness. The little chapel purrs with the echo of unintelligible but glorious Ave. The mauve, green, and red evening softly glistens in the large stained glass window of the nave. The first sighs blissfully, reflecting upon the dead tree, struck by lightning. "Good riddance, thank you my God. No more leaves to gather, to burn, what a deliverance!" The second wonders, "What more, or better could I have done this long day? What nobler, more perfect? I don't see..." As for the third, she still is not thinking. She savours the honey and the milk, the great love emanating from the statue of the protective Mother, her beautiful blue and gold guardian. And if she closes her eyes so affectionately, it is because under the plaster mask of Mary, she sees her own Mother again, the true one: all-powerful, infinitely gentle, generous with her warmth. The one whose skirts knew how to silently absorb the tears and secrets during the terrible, dissipated life before the taking of the veil. And then comes a great lull, altar of repose, benevolent limbo. Amen.

The mechanic's dog crawls under the Bédard's gallery, and rolls up into a ball. That is where I shall soon find him, curled up, trembling, with his empty eyes, his stiff paws, his emaciated tail, his fur all worn by the hard-packed dirt. He does not fall asleep immediately. Spasmodically, the cat returns behind his tired eyes. Now diving, now flying, now vanishing into thin air. The impossible cat, his tyrant. His deep woe, his physical despair, will move to tears the small, nosy, brotherly boy I shall be. I shall understand, I alone shall understand, and he will follow me all the way to the white house, without surprise, limping, already almost happy, as if he were entering dog heaven led by an indulgent little angel, after this long life in a purgatory plagued by rheumatism and despotic cats.

For a moment – catnapping, literally – my friend is brooding over his painful day. And it is as if, with him, at the same time as him, from deep in my limbo, I was glimpsing a multitude of elusive cats, through the fog of a fever. That's because I too am already being tugged at by the world. I too am thrown into the orbit of impossibility, I too enslaved and free, distraught, like my future best friend. Like him, already, everything is calling me and I need, blind, trembling, to live between my heart and the stars, frantic, hurried by time, awaited, predestined.

They are trying to sober up Sam. Gertrude, sitting in the hay, has taken his head on her thighs and is splashing rainwater on him, while Maurice examines the still from every angle while heaving out half-admiring, half-discouraged sighs. "Terrific gadget," he says, and bows his head as if he were facing the famous bomb dropped on Hiroshima whose murderous feats the newspapers lying around the old barn recount. My father will be fascinated and even excited all his life by cataclysms. Storms, picnics which end with a drowning, the Nuremberg trials on the radio, blizzards and ice storms which will confine uncles, aunts and cousins in the white house, monstrous forest fires. He will always be the first to clamber into his hip rubbers, untie the boat and leave to probe the lake for the drowned, or else fill the truck with men and take off full speed ahead towards the fire, bellowing out into the streets, "Fire!" He will have, at such times, too glowing a gaze, feverish panting like a big animal crazed with some instinct for combat, survival, or perhaps eternity. When he takes me on his lap to tell me about some disaster or another, I shall perk up my ears. But even before hearing, I shall guess, I shall quiver, me too, at the anticipated echo of the big, gruesome village rites. Gertrude, my mother, will stare at us scandalized, the way women, simply happy, stare at men tormented by misfortunes they cannot forget, by tragedies that, as she will say, "don't even happen to us personally."

Sam opens his eyes and closes them right away. He does not want to come back to the world. Limbo suits him just fine, so he says, "Leave me in peace." But Gertrude knows very well that Sam is not at peace in the slightest. "You're going to wake up, Sam, then come with us, big lazy-bones!" My mother laughs, saying that. She will often laugh while vociferating her reproaches, and that will mean, each and every time, "Nothing, not anything any more will be able to hurt us now. When you've gone through the persecuted youth your father and I have, nothing frightening can happen any more." And she will be right until the end, of course. Until the last morning.

They stand Sam up, and Maurice takes him on his back. Gertrude has opened the barn door and you can see the fields steaming after the rain, the setting sun smearing the horizon with blood, and the old Buick waiting, at the far end of the field.

Louis, perched high in his barber's chair, is smoking peacefully. The sky is red in his big shop window and Louis is smiling, his slender mustache, fully curved, makes a real face at him in the mirror. Just before heaving a big sigh and seating himself, Louis had turned the knob of his old radio. And now, the voice of his favourite singer, the great Charles Trenet, fills the room, Louis' heart, the village, the world. It is Louis' favourite time of day and it's also, by chance, his favourite song. How delightful life can be when it wants!

Un monsieur attendait
Au café du Palais
Devant un DuBonnet
La femme qu'il aimait...

Sipping a DuBonnet
at the Café du Palais
A gentlemen was waiting
For the woman he loved...

Louis settles into his chair, happy, while the smoke from his ciga-rette makes pink flowers, crimson hearts, scarlet faces in the air flooded with the setting sun, in his barber shop. "Happiness," thinks Louis, "is not all that difficult! No need to buy it with masses, come on!"

The crow has perched on the topmost branch of the oak, the same tree the two innocents had climbed to observe the mother bear and its young, before the storm. Now, the black bird, more blue than black after the rain, is crowing, meanly scratching the bark on the branch. Stretching its wings as if to fight or to protect itself, the crow sends forth piercing cries. Joseph Trépanier will call them "death cries!" And then it takes off, lumbering, tangled up for a moment in its flight, stiff-winged, its neck all in spasms like a turkey's throat just before the axe chops. First, it grazes the trees bordering the ravine, and then it lets itself sink, flowing into the blue shadows, diving towards the English marsh. Suddenly, its cries redouble: it sees them. Jacob has taken Germain on his back, as one does with a man who is too drunk or unconscious, and is carrying him painfully towards what seems to be a clearing beyond the brush. The crow lands on the summit of a dry elm and watches them. Its eyes are motionless, precise, almost ferocious with circum-spection. "Not that way!" At its strident, ear-piercing cry, Jacob turns around for a second, lifts his head towards the tree, the sky, nascent night on which he fixes his now useless eyes, his lost eyes, already full of death. He mumbles something like "Don't be afraid, my big cat, don't be afraid" to this friend on his back, to this heavy, hot, blood-stenched weight that, unknowingly, he is taking into the marsh.

They are going to plunge into the world over their ears. In vain we will search, dig, plunge into the sludge until we almost die too, we will only find a boot (Jacob's) crammed with mud and crayfish. Maurice will tell me a good dozen of their possible endings, each more frighten-ing than the others. I finally made up my own version and no one has contradicted my story yet, not even the crow who saw it all. But let us await night for the quicksand, for death imagined, in the English marsh.

Today you came with me to see Uncle Sam at the Asylum of Saint Michael the Archangel. You did not shiver at his glassy gaze, his leg which keeps shaking like the crank of some malfunctioning machine. You were nodding your head sympathetically at his dislocated, senseless sentences. He made you come right up to his bed. I don't know why: you began to talk to him about the child. He was touching your stomach. His big, beautiful, shivering hands were wrinkling your dress, looking for a sign, proof. You watched him serenely, without blushing. I left the room, upset. You joined me outside a few minutes later. You were quiet, smiling. You said to me, "He told me about you. He said that you knew how to listen like nobody else. That's beautiful, don't you think? I told him about the book. He is pleased, you know. As I was leaving, he pronounced the word 'to cross' or 'crossing,' I didn't quite catch it."

Crossing. He often used to say: "Life! What a crossing!" He would also say, "Lasting? What's the point of lasting?"

As we got into the car, you touched my arm and said: "Don't be sad, we're lucky, my love, both of us." Then I said, "The book... you must know that it is also because I'm afraid that everything will break, come undone, tear apart. But not the child. Him, he's for love, nothing but love." You smiled: "And so that nothing breaks, comes undone or tears apart. What harm is there in wanting his coming also to be for hope?"

My aunt Malvina waited out the storm in the attic. She will often take me up there, certain November days, when the weather is too bad to let me go outdoors and, especially, when her heart is too heavy with indelible memories. She will open the family album, the one she is clasping to her chest this very moment. In the candlelight appear old aunts in braids and lace, the old village boardwalk, the very first church that burned down, so much prettier than the others, the ones that came after it, couples in sleighs on frozen lakes, cousins snake-dancing on the main wharf, cousins in a joyous circle in the village meadow, cheerful picnics, proud weddings, grandmothers' faces shadowed by bell hats or veils, silhouettes of uncles returning triumphantly from successful fishing expeditions, their raised arms holding forth walleye and pike, smil-

ing and pale in the twilight. And then I turn a page too quickly.
"No! Not that one!"

"Who are those two? The man with his big hat pulled down over his
eyes? The young woman leaning on his shoulder and smiling so much
you can see her every tooth? But that's you, Auntie! And he's Sam! I recognize his big cat coat!"

At such times, my aunt will quickly close the album, her smile like
a harsh fold, her eyes moist, hands shaking. The attic will be her refuge,
her little nook, her chamber of beautiful, lost marvels. She will sit on the
bumpy old love seat, a vestige of those too long winter evenings, of her
fled youth, false engagement, unwise marriage proposals, treachery, lies,
solitude. The oak clock, with its broken hands, its motionless pendu-
lum, will continue to freeze time, to immortalize misunderstandings.
Even the wild cherry tree by the attic window will seem old, from
another era, a paralyzed memento, an immortal shadow, a mute, dis-
dainful witness to broken happiness.

Malvina rises, rubs and shakes her skirt, and now the dust of yes-
teryear, merging with the amber light of this evening in the attic of the
white house, completely melds seasons, times and chance, heartbeats
and haunting images. My aunt closes the trap door which makes a great
noise, as in church, or prison. On climbing back down the ladder, she
notices the bed in the bright room. The bed in which I shall be born, so
beautiful a bed, so sad. She enters, lights the little lamp, the one with the
spread-winged angel holding the light like a sheaf in its out-stretched
arms. "The bedroom is small," says my aunt aloud. And right after, as
though to stop her tears from flowing again, "But what are they doing?
They should already be here!" And then she goes back down to the
kitchen. Because to the kitchen one goes when one is anxious and one
has to move, forget, invent the rest of life, in the white house.

On my arm, I squash the mosquito that was harassing me. A tiny
speck of blood is swelling on my skin and, fast as lightning, the other

blood spurts forth again. The blood on the truck. The red, then brown and finally black stain, star-shaped, indelible. They had both been coming back from the doctor's.

Already Gertrude knew the terrible secret. The truck was not going very fast, it was an old truck. In the curve at the bottom of the hill, a deer leaped forth, then stopped right in the middle of the road, petrified by the engine noise. Maurice's full weight on the brake pedal was unable to stop the truck in time. A big heavy thud, and the beast fell stone dead, its antlers embracing the grill and the rusty old bumper. That spot of bright red blood on the front of the truck, when they got home. Gertrude explained, panting: the deer come out of nowhere, the useless brakes, the dust, the big, soft thud, an almost tender shudder, death, the horrible impression of having killed, the animal abandoned by the side of the road. The stain that grew brown in the sun and burned my eyes. Gertrude did not speak of the doctor, of the killer disease, of the secret. They must have spoken about it that night. I just stayed there, in front of the truck, hypnotized by the spot, dark red now, that sign, that omen. They called me from inside the house, I returned. Gilles, with his soothsayer's gift, might have been able to decipher that slash of blood, see their death, and prevent it? Three days later, they departed forever.

My love, I cannot continue the book. Not today. That old, swollen sign has reappeared. I rush down the stairs and find you on the beach. You immediately see the red star on my arm. You bring your lips to it. I come to you, and we roll in the sand, indestructible, eternal for a few miraculous seconds.

Later, I tell you: "I shall have to speak of their disappearance in the book. I feel I must." You nod your head, take my hand and say, "Probably, yes. But wait a little longer. You'll see, things will come to you at the right moment." Then I roll onto my back, beside you, absorbing the sky's blue like rain.

"It looks like she's losing it...," Reynald tells Sylvia and Marcel, his little sister and his brother, standing, dumbfounded, at the foot of the bed. And Reynald is right: his mother is indeed losing it. She is absenting herself from the bedroom, the house, the world and will not return except to roam about as a wild-haired, moaning ghost certain nights when the moon is full, foggy nights when the village meadow and the naked *sauvagesse* will reappear in the mad light of dream. Then Rachel will haunt her terrified children's sleep as they lie shivering in their beds. She will climb the stairs and go back down, utter blood-curdling screeches and go back to bed, absent again and for a very long time. Malvina will sometimes take me with her to see the madwoman, our neighbour, and I shall stay a little too long, each time, stupefied, my heart pounding at the spectacle of this empty body with its inhabited, frightful eyes. Once, I shall hear it utter its grasslands cry, its cry of night-time horror, and I shall vainly seek sleep that night, burrowing under the bedspread, panting breathlessly, blind, in quest of my own reassuring scent deep in the over-sized bed. And then I shall get up, the floor will creak, I shall go down to wake up Malvina who will tell me everything: Léopold's Indian, the recurrent dream of their accurst couplings, Rachel Bédard's madness. And that will be terrible, a sin, a malediction: I will feel evil little shivers of pleasure, my saliva will thicken beneath my tongue and I shall imagine all sorts of black delights beneath the moon. Rachel Bédard's fatal night will be my first night of sweat and fire, my first night of delicious shivers, my first night of desire and terror. I shall long believe that a superb demon, on horseback, was travelling through the area when the moon was full, looking for the big desirers, Léopold and company, and me with them, to demonize them with rage, pleasure and blood. I shall never be able to tell that, which will long eat away at me, to Gertrude, my mother, who would have hushed me. Nor meven to Maurice, although he would have understood me since he too was often sucked into whirlwinds of passion and wildness. Still less to Malvina who, her whole life long, will stay mute about her flames and fevers. She who will be obliged to turn her head away at the ambiguity of the slightest palpitating desire, not letting us see anything of her emotion but the hardened profile of a formerly passionate young girl.

"Dare to look beyond things! Dare to believe your own hands, your clear gaze that can touch the world yet leave it as is, not transform it, diminish it, destroy it," big Gilles will tell me. All washed with rain, set free by the storm, the big Métis has climbed back on Belle-Fille, his mare. There they are, climbing the mountain path. They are going to go watch daylight sinking, shipwrecked, into the big lake. Big Gilles will keep his eyes wide open, staring at the immensity until the earth pales and the first stars pierce the dark sky. The mare will not budge, being used to the daily whims of her master and friend. Both of them, in mute, proud reverence, in a deliberate trance, will stand out like totem silhouettes on the rocky ridge, way up there, motionless and solemn against the darkening sky. I shall often see them, as I raise my head from my school notes, from my so difficult books, Big Gilles and his mare, both arched against the red sky, insolent, magnificent. They will be my youthful figurehead, my way of the cross, my sphinx, my centaur, my first vision of such rare dignity. I shall often climb onto that same ridge, hoist myself onto a big, round-backed rock, on horseback in my turn, motionless too, unmoveable, aware of the majesty of the sky above me and the infinite tenderness of the sun on my face like a mask, no doubt a feeble imitation of the Métis' serenity, puny, perhaps, in the world, but in my turn solid, upright, powerful for a few dizzying seconds, tiny rider of infinite space.

We are driving along a road bordered by fields of alfalfa and clover. And then, just as we reach the top of a slope, begins the forest with its rows of giant pine trees. Suddenly, on your brown skin, tiny, rapid, spangled constellations appear, sparkle and vanish, as abruptly as reflections. As we climb, the lake becomes bigger and bigger, bluer and bluer, suddenly visible in its entirety, a gigantic spot of brilliant blue. Then you utter an "Oh!" like the little moan you make when you wound yourself (which is often) with cutting objects, knives, catnip, fishing line. A moan to say that it is almost too beautiful.

We turn right, towards the cove. On each side of the road appear old wooden cabins, wrecked cars, the poverty of the reservation, its cemetery-like silence, its desolation, like some abandoned park. The great grasslands, the old warpath. Paradise lost, henceforth a legend. Memories of hot coals, or of ashes, depending on the keepers of memories. According to my own childhood: hot coals. You say to me, "Tell me more about them, bring them back to life." I stop the car at the end of Huit-Anglais Road, from which you can see the whole hill above, the one where the story I want to relate took place. I take your hand, and a deep breath, and say: "See those rocks cutting into the shoreline so much they look like half of a tiger's wide-open mouth? Look closely. You see the big rocks in the water that push forward like a sort of wharf?" You answer yes, that you see them. So I go on: "The Indians had decided to build nothing less than a street on the water so as not to belong to the village. They could not and did not want to pay taxes, you understand. It involved the oldest, unchangeable, stubborn ones. They managed to put six cabins up on rock debris thrown into the lake, torn from the cliff with their bare hands. Six old Indian couples anchored out in the water, isolated, happy, tranquil." You say, "And then?" I continue: "And then there was an accident. On a foggy night, a boat strayed off course, crashed into the quay, destroyed the cabins, the old Indians. There was nothing left except that pile of old stones you see in the water." You ask me if the boat did it on purpose. I reply, "It was an accident. At least, that's what's always been said."

You look at the remains of what the villagers still call the "street on water." I can see you are moved. Perhaps I should not have. The wind is playing sadly in your hair. I ask, "Do you think you'll get used to it? Will you be able to live, like me, in this village between two worlds? Knowing what you know now, and happy nonetheless that all that did exist, still lasts, chipped, painful? That it all is a deeply-rooted, dangerous part of me?" You take the steering wheel. We go back the way we came. The lake disappears, the pines reappear, making stripes again on your arms, your face. You stop the car in front of the white house, and say, "Yes, I want to live all that with you. What's more: he too will know, and that will tear him apart, and help him grow."

You start up the car. You take our favourite road, the one along the water. No doubt you wish to unburden us of the painful weight of what did not happen, that too heavy weight of stubbornness and tenderness that fills our wings with lead.

And that will most surely put some in his too.

What is left of the sun, a big orange cloud, is shimmering through the pines. The whole village is visible in the lake, watery with its rippling houses, the church steeple like a ripe head of grass, the mountain above it with its waves of leaves glistening after the rain. The blazing depths of the sky give the village that look of pacified enchantment, that fairy-tale beauty that I shall so often see in it, evenings, on returning from fishing with Maurice, my father. A respite of moist gold, a lull, a sort of mirage. The village is gliding, fleeing. All is reflection, gleaming, and I shall often get the feeling that with a good wind, we could easily disappear off the earth. As though the village was not and had never been anything but a beautiful illusion invented by some dreaming god, and we but sluggish sleepers at the mercy of his changing dream, ourselves ephemeral, easy to erase.

Before my birth, even before being propulsed by love, tiny, burning, fluid spark of energy, into the passion of the big bed, I am already striving, this evening, attentive, curious, to outwit beforehand the fragility of appearances, the floating echo of the village, life's elusive current. I shall always want to see beyond, always want to capture the mad god's gestures, always seek to know why I too shall be that blind pilgrim, that mystery, that living, quivering creature hastening in pursuit of an ever-changing world, like its golden reflections in the big lake, like its clouds, like its seasons. And I shall never know, of course. Just as I do not know, this evening, before the night in the bright room, what makes life so dear, so reckless, so fragile, so enigmatic, so sure of itself, so urgent, so beautiful.

"That's the mountain, over there! That's it!"

Gertrude shouted, then she kissed Maurice, making him stray off the middle of the road. The Buick stops at the top of the big hill, the one I shall so often hurtle down, half fluttering bird, half terrified little boy, on my bicycle. Sam is still snoring on the back seat. My uncle Sam is not partaking of the honeymoon. He is alone in his limbo, sleeping off his whisky, curled up like a suffering animal. The newlyweds get out of the car, leaving the doors open so as not to disturb cousin Sam's troubled sleep. They have come to see the lake, the village, from afar, from above. Their arms around each other's waist. A double warmth makes them invulnerable, saved definitively: they have arrived, finally. "Look!" says Gertrude, "In the distance, over there, you can see the big bay!" Maurice says nothing. He nods his head. This beautiful, unfamiliar land, that bay blazing far off on the horizon, that brand new, thrilling mountain, that lake like a sea, this free life, this new world, are almost too much for him. After so long a wait, and now here it is, right in front of him, suddenly, this future, this silent village, this hope! He walks forward three steps along the road, alone. Gertrude lets him go. She can see his proud neck, his back, almost too strong, she clearly sees him brace himself in the road sand, feet set apart, his right hand raised to shade his eyes, his left hand on his hip, her husband, her freedom, her man gazing at the oasis, the hill, the end of this crazy honeymoon trip. She knows full well my father is crying. He is crying with relief but also with newness, obscurity, the sudden chill that comes when a goal is reached. He is crying softly, soundlessly. Then he returns to his wife, pulls her to him, holds her a little too tight, saying "I can't believe it, my love, I can't believe it!" And then, suddenly, a wave of warmth melts the little chill that was prickling between his ribs, like a ray of sun.

Now the Buick is heading down the hill, speeding towards the village, towards the big white house, on that same road you too took for the first time, not so long ago.

My hand, on your fair belly, is throbbing like a branch that has found water. You say: "Your head, put your head, your soft weight on my belly." Then I hear your marine world, I feel your strength, your warmth calming my eagerness, that mad rush towards joy, we know well which joy, a rush that never stops in my head. Once our skins are joined, round life begins anew, as, perhaps, already, the beginning of the child in you is curling up upon itself. And then I think, without saying it, "You and me, lose our taste for life, its touching chaos? Never, as long as we don't lose the knack. Amid our arms, our legs, there is a rhythm like a rushing river. We were afraid, like everyone. Then we outwitted fear and now we are dancing before the black tree. And then sparks burst forth in our eyes, like stars, in praise of the wonderful fate that made our bed. All is ready now, she can come. We're expecting her any day now."

Night

Perhaps I shall be both man and woman? I am already male and female and still more, aquatic and rapid, indefinite, ambiguous, because time does not yet exist. To choose is impossible. I am sinking, slipping into the burning tenderness of my mother's water. I am in turn hidden and revealed, little male, little female. I shall soon have branches and a snake of hard bone, I shall be a little, motionless, dizzy fish. But I shall also have wind in my bag, the skin of a Medusa, and my mother's blood, long opaque, will nourish me, will be my first pink lake, the colour of the autumn sky at dawn, and will taste of seas unknown. I shall be amphibious, ambivalent, ambiguous. I shall be like a spring swelling upwards deep in the rock: a broth saturated with spores and squirming with urgency, with the anticipated pleasure of guiding all these births to safe harbour. The soul too, my soul, bathed by the nourishing waters, will be now fluid, now firm, clear and cloudy like a brook before and after a gust of spring wind. I shall immediately recognize light, for I shall have had it, pink, filtered but gleaming, like an enveloping screen, a beautiful sign of life calling me, coiling round me, making me grow. Fusion, soft lights, a call. Like sunshine on the snow on the window of a bedroom with closed shutters. I shall not want to sleep much. I shall kick and punch. Sleep? When I can sense the abundance bursting forth outside, that life of light which Gertrude's skin will barely allow through, that new life, soon mine: sleep?

The darkness does not fool the mare, who knows her way by heart. First, she and her rider will pass in front of the church. The big Métis will doff his hat, and whoever sees him will seriously doubt the courtesy of his gesture and especially his Christian fervour. Then they will stop a moment beside the lake, on the dike by the presbytery. Big Gilles will let his mare drink. He too will drink, on horseback. He is drinking the evening splendour. From where he is, he can see the mountain fading out in the lake and the lights on the far shore appearing like stars. You can see the vast sky as from nowhere else, a beautiful wool-grey, loosely woven with the sunset's last frothy red threads. You can also see the whole bay sinking into the brown of the night lake and the infinite brown sky, so mingled that one cannot tell if the big beach, for example, might not be the clear, sparkling crescent of a star come to brush the village, so as to touch the "night owls" sitting on their verandas, at twilight. You can also see the edge of the water lighting up the night a little, as though a light was on above the thousands of phosphorescent scales on the backs of the wall-eye come to sleep in the warm water. And you can feel and breathe, there and only there, the scent of the world's beginning that Big Gilles recognizes well, and that calms desires and longings better, far better than the priest's prayers and incense (the priest has not seen Gilles because the priest is already asleep, because he is dreaming, in his great, princely presbytery, of mysteries supernatural).

And then they will go back up the hill, both appeased, until they disappear into pitch black, the great, grassy night.

I shall never know if he is sleeping, or out of breath, or has died in his sleep, that mechanic's dog. His rough hair stirred by the night wind like dead grass on top of a rock, his snout in the ground like a little field mouse damp with fever, motionless and mysterious, he is asleep under the Bédard's porch, lying there, abandoned again and as always. Anxiety is taking advantage of his exhausted sleep. It is slinking into his blood. All his cells, unflinching, are slowly poisoned by shadows full of blinding images, different and yet always the same, since it is always one and the same image: the fleeing cat, despairingly rust-coloured and beautiful, infinitely free and scornful. It is ever the same fencepost, the same terrible, dazzling sky, the same maddening leap, the same red flash, the same bitter saliva under his tongue and finally, the same sudden awakening, a shock, a spasm, electricity stiffening his limbs, making him whimper in the dark and strike his head against the planks of the veranda, lost, frantic, so alone, the mechanic's dog.

There he goes, off wandering again, shivering, blind, in the middle of the main street, beset by the same, good old bitter delirium, regretting despite himself the cat's nocturnal absence, missing that beautiful, rust-coloured, inseparable enemy spending its night where it is warm, as is sensible. He raises his head, looks for the moon to bite into, to unleash his howl, seeking delivery. But the village is pitch dark, the end of the world, limbo.

Malvina has lit the lantern and gone out onto the porch. As far as the beach in front of the white house, the yellow light stretches forth huge shadows with glowing streaks. Moths, bees, and a few precocious mosquitoes come and get a fright, banging against the lantern in frustration, suicidal, the poor things, because they are madly in love with the all-powerful flame of my aunt Vina's little lantern. You can hear the frogs croaking, their love song mingling with the woodchucks', and, in the cove reigns a hymn, a joyful, great sigh swelling the night with desire. A gentle breeze brings scents. The scent of new earth, of moss at the shoreline, and the cooler, soothing scent of open water. A light fog is rising. So rich a night takes Malvina by surprise. My aunt is standing upright, at the top of the stairs, in her beautiful black dress, the one she has had for ages, breathless, motionless, with her shadow wavering on the grass. She is ready to welcome the newlyweds, and their being late is making her anxious. "What a beautiful night," my aunt thinks, "What a beautiful night they'll have, the lucky pair!" And then she sighs, pleased with this sudden joy in her breathing. Our happiness, Gertrude's and Maurice's and later mine, will also be her happiness. We do need it, you cannot live without happiness. However difficult it may be to spot. And moreover, Malvina has not reached the end of her surprises, nor of her expectations.

Above the bay the tufted ducks are passing back and forth. Silently, like conspirators. Soon they are going to split up, shed the heavy weight of their travels and head deep into the creeks to nest. All is in order, ready, the world is ready as a nest. Already, you can hear the old Buick coming up the cove road.

The first one went to bed right after the prayer she murmured off by rote. Fresh sheets, silence, the lovely abyss of night will be blissful rest. Tomorrow there will be so much to do, the universe is still in disorder, the Kingdom is not yet, alas, of this world, it will take hard work. And then she falls asleep, exhausted by her future sacrifices. The second one is raging at the big fly prowling about the crucifix over the head of her bed. "Did you ever see such impertinence?" She brandishes her hand and arm in the air, but in vain: the fly intends to wear itself out at its pleasure, wander about to its heart's content, wildly, all night long. It has just awakened from its long winter, its numbing torpor. "The innocent creature does not understand its sin," thinks the little nun, sighing. And then she puts the sheet over her head, hoping to forget the sacrilegious insect. But the buzzing is even worse, an obsessive, fatiguing reminder of paganism eternal, of the world's cruelly unending barbarity, poor us! "Oh, no! Not another sleepless night," thinks the little nun, "not another night suffering from the savagery here below." She is suffocating under the sheet. So she emerges, poking her head out grumpily, and the whole process must begin anew: say her prayers, try to calm down, beg trust in God, find peace once more. Salvation, that thorny rose on the tip of its long branch!

As for the third, she is asleep. Dream quietly regains possession of her forgotten body. The big Métis' horse, its moist, overwhelming muzzle, its strangely soft heat. Oh! Such nice, forbidden torpor, the delicious, forbidden shivers! In the depths of her dream, there is something... yes, heavenly: surrendering your will to that superb beast that knows so well how to surprise you, remove your scruples, conquer you. During a long, infinitely soft second, your whole body quivers as though it was flying away, and then she knows nothing, the third little nun, she no longer knows anything sad, nor tired.

She lies there, blissful, rested, fulfilled, innocent.

She is the one who will teach me, in a few years, to look out the classroom window to find human shapes in the clouds, to count the gulls (how many with a yellow beak, how many with black wing tips?), to know which way the wind is blowing, and she will explain the blue of the sky, why it rains, what makes fireflies glow and also a little grammar and nebulous arithmetic. She will be very seriously troubled the day I ask her, "Did that nasty Indian that ate the missionary's heart, Father Jogue's, go on living afterwards with two hearts in his chest?"

We are walking on the beach in front of the white house. I am continuing to teach you this new world. I tell you of the patience and stubbornness and confidence it took to preserve the beauty, the mystery of this shore. You bend your head at each memory flushed out and which immediately captivates you. Is it the mingled flavours of the brand new and the permanent that makes you breathe so deeply, that charms you like a delighted traveller and makes me tell once again the anecdote, the myth, the legend, the aura of this beach, our new beach?

As we approach the big wharf, you notice something, a sort of date or graffiti engraved in the cement. "What's that sign, that drawing?" I answer, "It's a ship sinking. Over there to the left, you can see the wide-open mouth of a frog that's going to swallow the vessel. And up above, a fire, the fire of vengeance that will burn the sailors." You look at me, confusion in your eyes. "But what does it mean? It looks like Inca or Maya hieroglyphics." I answer, "You're almost right. The Indians built this wharf for the whites. They made sure they left a prayer on it, an evil spell. You see, they built this wharf truly despite themselves, on the site of their former landing spot. They built the masters' wharf, but they certainly did not wish them bon voyage. The sign did not appear until the stone covering the cement was eroded off." You shake your head, then ask, "And were there any shipwrecks?" I smile: "Many. So many that for a long time, shipping came to a halt. Boats did not begin to descend the river again until the Indians finally got their beach back, two miles downstream."

Almost ceremoniously, you touch the lines hollowed into the cement. You say: "It's absurd. I just had an absurd thought." You lean your back against the warm cement, covering half the drawing. All that remains visible is the incantatory blaze above your head. Suddenly, you become very pale, and say, "What if our world proves not to be right for him? I mean, when all these eroded old stones fall, he too will discover the dangers, the traps." I touch your hair, you have closed your eyes, you are struggling with the image of our child betrayed by the world, by us, driven from Eden, discovering lies. Then you smile, look at me, "Those are a pregnant woman's thoughts, don't you think?" I take your hand, and we walk together for a long time, until night falls. You bring back a big, night-blue oyster shell that you say will stop the papers on my table from flying off.

It is very windy, and you are sleeping. The child will inevitably be betrayed, my love, we cannot help it. But aren't some betrayals beautiful?

Already, I am those shivers on their skin, that beautiful, pure desire, the heat of their panting. I cannot resist the foretaste of their wedding night, like light dissipating the mists of limbo. Oh! That trembling haste!

They are holding each other tight. The Buick is parked beside the lake, right near the stand of bulrush with its good smell of summer, pleasure as perfume in the evening air. They are enjoying each other audaciously, simply. I am their bursting desire. I am this time they are taking, while deliciously ignoring time. I am their saliva, their sweat, their mingled breathing. I am the almost painful cry of the bittern in the nearby marsh. I am that brand-new night mystery gliding upon them like a veil, silently. I am that effervescence in their veins, that slightly painful haste, their wish to last forever like that, fulfilled, escaped, free. They are kissing, and I am that kiss lasting and filling them with a perfect, round joy, that rejoicing that will soon bring me forth.

Down at the road's end, Malvina and the big white house await us. Sam, meanwhile, is still sleeping on the back seat of the Buick, absent, damaged, plunged into that same nothingness I am leaving with all the energy I can muster.

Not far from there, leaning against the frame of his door wide open to the night, Louis the barber is smoking, thinking. The same ideas always float around the notion of well-being, that sort of secret charm that wide open eyes, derusted ears, unplugged nostrils and especially a simple heart are able to give to a willing person. It is to him I shall go to confess my sun-drenched sins, the first ones, my frenzies, like itches, always sure that I shall find Louis attentive, interested, smiling affectionately. Louis, so far removed from anything treacherous or spiteful, like a stranger in his place in the world, alone, pure as his deep gaze. He will often be able to recognize, in everyone, our sometimes muffling solitude. Mine, consisting in being trusting by taste, impressionable by nature and joyful out of necessity. Louis will always welcome speech, whether it expresses suffering or enthusiasm, ardour or distress. Bilious or fiery conversations in his bright barber shop, a sort of confessional without absolution or penitence. The speaker is on his chair, comfortable or timid, bold or scrupulous, and the listener standing behind him is attentive, smiling, they are both implacably reflected in the big mirror facing them. Constantly confronted with himself, the speaker will leave Louis' barber shop relieved, often determined to break the bad spell, or to consent to its all too tempting nibbles. All this, without philosophizing or moralizing. Simply with that rare depth, Louis will encourage the blooming of a passion, or its rejection, escape from tension, flight from danger or, most often (and this will quite suffice), confession of some numbing fear or a great, stubborn, fearsome desire. People will always feel soothed after a visit to Louis' barber shop.

For the moment, Louis is smoking, staring at the night, easily avoiding the anxiety such infinite obscurity contains, delighted with his fate, moved by the beautiful summer just beginning, and alone, so much so that he does not mind talking aloud, or even singing what he calls his own special prayer:

Ah si l'amour prenait racine
Dans mon jardin, j'en planterais
J'en planterais, j'en sèmerais

Aux quatre coins
J'en ferais part à tous mes amis
Qui n'en ont point...

Oh, if love took root
In my garden, I would plant it
I would plant it, I would sow it
In every corner
I would share it with all my friends
Who have none...

"Even without love," thinks Louis, "we love, we can love. Come on, it's not so difficult!"

Gone insane, Rachel Bédard will turn her nights into her days. An innocent and dreadful prowler, she will wander about the garden, by the lake, through the streets until the wee hours, haunting the village with the macabre memory of Léopold and the Indian woman, found together in their bed of accurst spruce branches.

She has risen, gone down to the beach. Her children are sleeping, they do not yet know the monstrous fable that is just beginning. Malvina sees her skipping on the beach stones, hears her muttering ardent invectives to the night. Little cries, growls that seem to come from the marsh, the sky, elsewhere. And then my aunt sees Rachel's eyes lit up by the harsh light of the little lantern she is holding. A scourge, a cataclysm: the eyes of an escaped lynx, mad, blazing eyes. Eyes that recall the horrors of yore: wild animals battling in the grasslands, Indians drowning in the cove, loggers suffocating, sick with scurvy or moonshine and other black magic out of old tales. Rachel Bédard's eyes have become enraged. The whites completely fill the orbits and shine like fireflies. My aunt raises the shawl on her shoulders, unable nonetheless to calm the shivers running over her body. She goes down the veranda steps and follows Rachel onto the beach. But the mad woman flees, plunging into the night, screaming like a wounded cat.

Suddenly, you cannot hear anything, see anything. Rachel Bédard's ghost has disappeared. A bad dream vanished. Little Reynald comes out onto the gallery in his pyjamas, rubbing his eyes. He is trembling, he does not know what the world is coming to.

"Mummy!"

The cry brings Rachel out of the shadows. She is now a quiet spectre, a fallen, mute hallucination, a monster emptied of its weirdness. Freed from her rage as if by enchantment, Rachel takes Reynald by the arm, leans on him and climbs the stairs, puffing, as after exertion, on returning from the garden or from a good run on the beach, no more, no less. Only the mist her wild breathing traces in the air still stupefies my aunt Vina, who watches Rachel go into her own house and cannot get over it, will never get over it. The little lantern trembles, and makes a big, unrecognizable shadow tremble behind it.

I shall often go down to the beach, at night, abruptly awakened by the terrifying wails of Rachel Bédard, mad woman, haunted widow. I shall even follow her once, as far as the dam on the turtle-filled river. Her undone nightgown, billowing in the night like some huge bat over the water. I shall see her withered breasts, like two drifting islands, her belly torn by claws, her claws, and hear her curse God, heaven, the world and above all, above all, the Devil's squaw. She will stamp on the dam until she almost falls off, drowns, perishes, in a sort of bewitching, possessed dance. And, despite my goose flesh become hawk flesh, I shall be unable to wrest my gaze from that furious apparition, so strangely beautiful, from that peninsula of flesh and veils, haranguing the night like a tortured priestess. Curiously, it is on a night like this that the word "fate" will arise spontaneously in me. A word that will ever remain crazy, said, repeated, sometimes screamed by the cracked voice of a mad woman flying off into the night.

Later on, my love, they will try to make me understand that, on one side of my skin is God, and on the other, me, and that He and I shall never be able to meet. So this God will never meet my heart, my lungs, my brain? Nor the trees beneath their bark, nor a butterfly in its cocoon? I shall know they are lying. I am a bit of that God, a spark escaped from an ever-exploding sun freeing stars that long remain incandescent. Their God will not be mine. In my limbo, God is male and female, perceptible, tangible. S/he is endless desire and also its coming fulfillment, both mysterious and certain. The asphyxiating peace of churches, a heaven ever promised, hoped for, but never desirable, the separation of the world into good and evil, between wise acts and mad acts, between sapwood and bark: not for me. I shall not belong to the herd of grace-deprived creatures seeking forgetfulness. Right here and now are sufficient passion, appetite, expectation and satisfaction: life. I already am infinitely convinced that no longer being in death will be quite enough. Enough to triumph, even in pain. Enough to love, even in doubt. Enough to not want to return to death in any hurry. Neither philosophy nor moralizing. A certainty of limbo and soon of flesh, a red, throbbing belief: I am coming out of death, propulsed, aware only of what comes after limbo, this insubordination to the laws of the priests and the obtuse, this limpidity without indulgence nor pardon, this soaring out of night, this sometimes wrenching flash, this god: daylight.

The owl is crying its lugubrious two-note groans, like a liturgical chant. Perched high on the top of the tallest spruce, it sees all. Night has no secrets for it. Neither does the English marsh. It was born here, lives here, hunts here, raises its brood here, and will die here. It will outlive the two innocents who are going to sink into moving death, into the marsh sands that suck you down and drag you, like someone drowning, to the centre of the earth by your hands and feet.

Jacob has hobbled to the oak at the edge of the accurst pond, near Joseph Trépanier's, just before the apple orchard begins. He had caught a glimpse of Germain's torso and especially his head of mud and moss, unrecognizable, a hateful mask still stirring, but like the shadow of a shadow, no longer puffing, no longer shouting, perhaps no longer alive. And then darkness fell suddenly, filling all the holes in the forest with thick, viscous ink smelling of sludge. Jacob struggled along until he was breathless on his branch that finally breaks, tearing something else in the night, something like the hope contained in the branch itself. "Too late," says Jacob's voice within Jacob, his voice caught in the sand, a voice that is sinking, drowning in its turn. And then the pain came back, when Jacob fell with the branch. Enough for the innocent to pass out for a last, fatal moment. Come to his senses, or rather to what was left of him, Jacob crawled as far as the reeds, where, if you go forward by one more elbow, you immediately begin to be swallowed up by the monster disguised as a moist beach. There Jacob glimpses, half snake, half ghost, his cousin's face, his white eyes, his mouth palpitating like a fish out of water, his hair tangled, twisted, little grass snakes gleaming in the thick darkness around him. "Big cat," says Jacob's now toneless voice, "big cat, big cat, wait for me!" Germain's mouth spasms horribly, then closes, mute cavern. All you can see are the bluish whites of the eyes in the mud-covered face trying to say "Jacob, you idiot, you sucker, run, go away, run, come back with men and ropes, you innocent!..." But already Jacob, suffering reptile, is crawling, advancing dangerously to the edge of the big broth brandishing the trembling, pathetic oak branch vainly dangling like a spider over the swirl. "Jacob, back up, go away!" scream the phosphorescent eyes in that face of mud. And then, as though coming from elsewhere, from the forest along the edge or perhaps an owl's throat, a single, hoarse, macabre shout: "No!" Echoes repeat the useless clamour ten times and then, nothing. The deafening torpor of the marsh, humming like a malaria-ridden trap, its small, moist, man-eating noises, greedy and very calm, its mushy breathing, its discreet stench. The branch immediately began to tremble like a water-seeker, then dove, dragging with it the arm and shoulder, in a flash. As for the legs, they were somehow soothed on entering the coolness of the clayish sand, especially the mutilated knee. A sort of merciful well-being, before the end. All that remains is the head, a twin to the other but still clean, not yet muddied. Cousin Jacob's light face, petrified, with a sort of fervour in its eyes, comes within two feet of cousin Germain's caked, horrible face, to await death, to be swallowed into a burial of mud and muck. The two innocents stare at each other and, slowly, descend together into swampy death. Can they hear the owl screech, the wind mourning them, the bull frogs, puffed up like drowned corpses themselves, glorifying summer, fertility, the flavours of the English marsh, abundance, life? Can they hear all those wild songs that are the opposite of death, that are innocence, freedom? Are they not already on the other side of mystery, in limbo? Are they not brushing me with their clay-smooth limbs, their wizard's hair? Are they not passing by right now, here, an oak branch away from me, from my curled up, formless entity vibrating with their fresh death?

I shall often go to wander on the shore of the English marsh. Gertrude will never know about it. Only to Maurice, my father, great lover of horrible tales, shall I be able to speak of my fascination with whirlpools, of how I tremble with voluptuous shivers, that sort of dark, breathless pleasure. And even to him, not everything. Not the jostling images that they will give birth to in me and that will have to await books, poems and films, many years, before finding their confidants, equal in guilty terrors.

As for Jacob and Germain, the two innocents, I shall often believe that their two souls are reunited in my body. As if, having seen them pass by so close to me as they were leaving the world and I was on the verge of entering it, like drowning people touching one another in the current, I was going to be born with my own distinct form, my sovereign body intact, but with their two trembling, fatal lights in my soul. I shall often think of myself as double, a big cat and a shy worshipper of big cats, both Jacob and Germain, doubly innocent, and dizzyingly fascinated with death by eddies and whirlpools, disguised as a tree-sheltered beach in the English marsh. Indeed, one day when I am stupefied and unhappy to be on this earth and to be double, to find no room for either part of the double innocence in me, I shall go to the marsh and long for a permanent, gentle, cool disappearance. A desire for mud and nothingness, for that centre of the earth which to me will never be hell, but rather a well-deserved rest of roots, clay and precious stones.

Another night, the same night – ours. We are stretched out on the beach in front of the white house, gazing at the sky. I have made a fire. Twigs rise, briefly imitate stars, then streak downward, go out before they reach the water. Orion is staring down at us, the Big Dipper is within arm's reach. All those shimmering stars are making us pleasantly dizzy. We both seem to be waiting. We are patient, red with firelight moving, dancing over our faces with their wide-open eyes. We are full of tenderness, it is flowing from all over us. Tenderness flows from us like sweat. If you touch me, I'll burst, I'll splash all over. If I touch you, you hollow out, then you turn into a volcano, a nest of hot coals. We are making our baby tonight, I could swear to it. He will have summer blood, the soul of a starry night, a skin of sand, river eyes, mountain scent. He will be fever and snow, like our desire. He will be a bird with wings wide stretched, tree and grass, he will be breeze and sky. He will be sensitive, pure, vibrant. I enter you: he will be a fish at play, a whirling sky, a gust of wind, spasm, torrent. You turn me over and mount me: he will be a rider, male and female, a black, shiny fairy, she will be as firm as a vice grip, marsh, river, ocean.

As I get my wind back, your own breathing gradually slows. We are again slick with pleasure, dazzled and brand new. Still flushed, you say, "That's what I call leaving nothing to chance!" And then you lean your head back, your lips shine, you are fertilized by so many stars that there is sure to be one for him.

We go back up to the bedroom. The nighthawk splits the pure black of night, freeing a tiny, burning joy that endlessly begins anew. I slide my hand down to your throbbing genitals and say, "My love, I am not dreaming, I'm not loony or enigmatic. I know full well we are simply ambiguous spaces traversed by world history. I also know that joy is difficult, ours and the nighthawk's with its passion and nocturnal melancholy. The fact is, we can't know peace except when we're running, or we get carried away. Motionless and dreaming, we shipwreck, we don't last, we sink. I know, I stagnated a long time, you know it too. But ever since you came and lit this love that has so quickly come to the forefront, I know I'm free, I've escaped, fast, totally appeased. I shall never cease celebrating your coming, my cure, hope. So I'm sure about her too. I know she will experience this race, this searing beginning, this second birth. And then she'll soar, make her way in life, fly off."

I tell you that I can feel her right by, so close she will prevent me from sleeping. You listen to my ravings, laughing, your sunlit head on the pillow. I go on talking to you, wildly, words counting less than my excited breathing, the surging overflow. "I'm certain that, when we're born, we complete the form that was given to us by the old, worn-down world's desire to burst. Then we have to live that battle between sand and river, keep it up, that beautiful battle that has no goal, that suffices unto itself." I pick up the plover egg that you brought back from your afternoon walk. I say, "Look at the pattern of brown spots on the eggshell. It's never the same on any two eggs. That shows you, right away, overwhelming, limitless immensity! The mystery of passions is not biblical at all. We could try in vain, so as to exorcise the heart, soon the child's, for example, we could try in vain to tear it from your womb, dissect it, destroy its network of nerves and fats and examine it under a microscope: we could never discover the thousand tendernesses you would have to penetrate, like a little snake of light, to understand and be aware of what the sum total of its identical, repeated beats really means. If you want to know, to bless and forgive, don't rack your brains, sing!" You say, "Come to bed, Khalil Gibran!" But I continue, and you laugh even more. All that matters are satisfied curiosity and disappointed curiosity. The terrible flavour of the world is sometimes a torture as painful as a Way of the Cross. My love, the child is singing her passion deep within you, I can hear it! You laugh and I hug you so tight I can hear your heart in my chest. You say, "You'd best get back to work." And you are still laughing. I say, "You're right. I shall finish soon, my love, soon finish."

Curled up like a sleeping hound dog on the back seat of the Buick, my uncle Sam is sleeping off his moonshine whisky. A binge is ending, and his heart is returning to him intact, chaotic, sad. An old, frustrated, miserable dream is surfacing with the familiar trees along the road and the sky he vaguely recognizes overhead. Now and then he is stricken with nausea as the potholes and bumps come and go. My uncle will often relate to me the tale of this backwards journey. Budging his violet cheeks in that strange nodding he will display while saying "If I had left, little guy, I might have seen New York or even California, who knows, whereas this village is the beginning and the end of the world, entangled, motionless..." Among all imaginable departures, all possible trips around the world, that mythical voyage will always remain his missed salvation. The arrival of the newlyweds who caught him, the way fate had thwarted his pathetic freedom were, and will remain, the bitter signs that an evil genie does exist, god or demon, pushing this way and that the unfathomable genetic reflexes of the hobo, the poor, highway-haunted madman. My old uncle will spend his whole life sleeping off his wedding whisky. For he will age quickly, bile under his tongue and the whites of his eyes shot through with blood paled by yet again a lot of whisky. Malvina's love, devotion and storms will be unable to free him from the distress of the great traveller stopped in his drunken course. Thanks to his voluble bitterness, I shall have the right to tales whose exact, studied geography will place the most beautiful countries on the village edge or at the end of the lake, so near and so fabulous, at any rate, all these enchanted, exotic sites, that, bicycling, I shall long be unable to believe my stupor as the unchanging forest endlessly advances towards me, without minarets nor palm trees nor golden caravans almost melting beneath the searing sun, no matter how far I go along the road leaving the village. Yet all those countries will exist as described, but so far away that I shall not see them all; it would take me three lifetimes to visit them all. That splendour, so close and out of reach, that uncle Sam will tell me about, will give me the soul of a traveller but a motionless one, in my turn. Alone and already departed, I shall often open the successive issues of my uncle's *National Geographic Magazine* and, Sam's shadow on my heels, I shall penetrate the burning Orient or frozen Arctic, the Amazon full of terrifying reptiles where beings decorated all over shall await me, their long-horned cattle behind them, so beautiful that, just touching the paper (glossy though it was), I shall experience a delicious fright, as though I were touching their silky, quivering hair. Camels and vultures, big and small salty seas, colourful vegetation, black men and women with proud, frizzy-haired heads, rice paddies with bowed, fervent Chinese or Indonesians labouring at the world's most beautiful work, sailing ships of the high seas and orchards in Ohio: that paper world, visited and re-visited, will enchant my winters, in the attic of the big white house. I shall owe my first awakenings, my only, immobile travels, to uncle Sam.

Sam is waking up. Rubs his eyes with one hand and his stomach with the other. The Buick is climbing the little slope. On seeing the white house and Vina, standing on the last step of the veranda, Sam splutters, "I'm dreaming, right? For sure I'm dreaming!"

My aunt has raised the little lantern she is holding out. The Buick stops at the foot of the big staircase. Gertrude runs up the stairs two at a time and there she is, hugging Vina breathless.

"I thought you would never get here!"

"I'll tell you, cousin, that was not your average honeymoon trip!"

"My God, your dress is stained all over! Where in the world have you been?"

"Wait, wait!"

Maurice has remained at the foot of the staircase, solemn, dusting off his suit, waiting. The two women come downstairs, hand in hand.

"Vina, he's the one!"

"Oh! It's you!"

"It's me!"

My father is smiling as he doffs his hat. My mother and my aunt are laughing, arms around each other's waist. Vina hugs Maurice as though they had been separated by a war or a long illness. Over my father's shadow, she sees Sam, in the car.

"What are you doing here?"

"Me? I'm not here. You musn't think I'm here, Vina. I'm dreaming and so are you."

Gertrude grabs the little lantern, freeing Vina from it, but my aunt does not budge.

"Well, kiss, for God's sake!"

Neither of them stirs. They are watching each other as though, indeed, they really were not there. After a long while, Sam decides to come and take my aunt's hand which he presses to his neck like a frightened little animal.

"I won't stay, Vina. They forced me to come back."

"Don't talk nonsense. Come on!"

All four of them enter the white house. They leave the lantern outside, at the top of the stairs. It lights up the night, the Buick, the suitcases at the bottom of the stairs.

You can hear laughing, and then Gertrude's voice emerges. She is telling of her trip, the adventure, her new freedom.

A strong wind is blowing. You have put a big log on the fire. You are looking at me, aware that I am hesitating. Is it time to write about it, now that our night has become similar to theirs, their wedding night? Is it time to speak of their death? You say, "Yes, tonight, right away, you must." A strong wind is blowing, and my old despair is beating its wings, exhausted. Gertrude and Maurice did not depart like so many others, from a long disease or a road accident. They committed suicide. I was fifteen. I was in mourning for more than twenty years. Their death explains everything, according to the psychiatrists: my wanderings, my silence. One even said, "If terror remains secret, it can go mad." What did these fans of terror know? The wind is screaming in the chimney. I do not want this crisis, rising, roaring like the wind outside. Their double disappearance, out on the water, in Maurice's row boat. Things aren't that simple. For over twenty years I have been fleeing the beach, the village, the legend. I had lost them both, forever. I am sure the psychiatrists would explain the book very well. The book itself will be proof of that soaring, buried madness. I can hear them: "That violent desire to embellish everything, to turn life into enchantment, that's a disease trying to ignore itself, it's dangerous!" Repressed, banished, terror turning itself into enchantment? Could we find the words to reject the hurt, that impossible pain? They frightened me for a long time with their almost sensible proclamations. And then I doubted, you came, I returned here. Our legend was unexpected, it changes everything. My love, don't stay on the bed. Come to me. Listen: they get into the row boat. Saying nothing, serious, calm, Maurice picks up a little metal recipient and bails out the rain water. Gertrude sits on the back bench, pale, sovereign in her dark decision. Why? My nights full of curiosity, my unhealthy nights have been so long. Why? Her letter said, "Because your father is ill, very seriously ill. I could not go on without him, my son. I told him the doctor had seen the disease, had condemned him. He has decided to die, and I with him. I want to follow him, you understand, follow him..." Was that terrifying enough? Cavalier enough? Their departure in a row boat in the middle of the night, their silent navigation as far as the Barque Isle channel. For a long time, I was behind them, in the row boat's wake, hanging on to an oar, breathless, useless. The landscape sank. That was the end of crazy summers, blissfully warm autumns, sparkling winters. The bay of childhood, and its immortality: finished. Too quickly came shame and battles, forced amnesia, lies, alcohol, flight. My love, turn on the lamp, stand up straight in the world's middle, watch me madly lighting up the labyrinth. Their death in the black water, their love death. Mine, right afterwards, on the beach, then in my nightmares, my death of horror. More than twenty years spent brooding on those two deaths, while pretending to work, conquer, drink, try my rotten luck. Then you came. They returned with you. Un-drowned, floating on the lake, following the row boat's wake backwards, walking on the water, they reached the wharf, entered the big white house, walking calmly, leaning on each other. Unchanged, alive. False drowning, pretend death to scare, disappearance in a child's dream, the absurd terror of an imaginative little boy. It is going to rain, you can smell the sand. The leaves are showing their pale side, they're upside down, panic-stricken. I love you. The child will be them again, them started anew. I will not have this fit. I no longer have fits. I now have only glimpses, sometimes shocks, an oppressed feeling similar to those you will soon experience because of him. Look, the sky is moving, the sky is turning, the storm is going to strike. Your fire is superb. All I want now is the silence back in the bed-room, their silence, ours. It is not about forgetfulness, pardon, nor even resurrection. It's about us both, all three of us, and the beautiful storm on its way. You come close to me, very close.

You kiss me in the neck, and say, "We never really talked about it. We won't ever again." You take me by the hand. We go near the fire. Yes, nothing left except, sometimes, glimpses, quiverings, shocks like those you will soon experience because of him. You undress me. You are very strong, very gentle, brown and red, you begin it all again, so simply. It is behind us now. The child has begun, the world is anew the world, the new world. Summer has come to light on your body, on mine. We have put it all behind us. It just had to be said, be written. It is finished.

It is like the sea, like in the sea I shall not discover until much later. I am a little algae transported by the waves. In its vast breathing, a danc-ing little spot. One day, in twenty years, I shall dive, and immediately recognize the brilliant coral, the hairs erect with moist sunlight, the old sand bottom strewn with jewel-like, sculpted seashells, the turquoise stripes swimming between two moving mountains of deep blue and also the beautiful mauve abysses where now and then a diamond gleams: the gilded flank of a barracuda, or silvery mother-of-pearl phosphorescence. I would not be at all surprised if salt was burning my eyes. My limbo eyes are closed, my eyes of the almost-born. Blind, I see with blood; I can see the diaphanous skin of my world; I can see with my salty eyes as I shall see underwater. Suddenly, inundated with a foam that I also recognize, but which burns me, I curl up in a moving mus-cle; I rush at her heart, flow back right away, half suffocating. Rolled up into a ball, wrapped in that white rain trembling on me, communicat-ing its spasms to me, I painfully accept what is happening. A tide hits, spreading over me, I am floating, lost. Then a new, wild fire cooks me to the core: small, boiling fruit, I shiver, deliciously thunderstruck. Much later, an airplane in the sky above me will break the sound barri-er. Curled up in the grass, on the beach, I shall recognize my father's roar, his energy breaking the old world, his din freeing me. If I already had a mouth, my first cry would immediately tear open the envelope, would liberate my waters sullied with this white liquid piercing me, killing me, changing everything too quickly. I have returned to the wave now, it contains me and does with me what it will, it will drown me if I do not begin to quiver too, twist, take up room, burst forth in the stormy water. But I cannot. I am a petrified little tadpole, overwhelmed with spasms, but motionless. Suddenly, without a blow nor a jump, here I am on a beach, swollen like a jellyfish the last wave just threw onto the sand, and I am breathing with my whole skin, I am full of this new, double blood. I am alone. Finally, I am alone. I am terribly alone. Alone, but changed, new, bigger, taller. From the troubled waters, in my middle, something is emerging. A thin, coral twig breathing for me, drinking blood for me, branching before my very eyes. One evening, much later, I will see a flower open, in slow motion, on a big screen: that will be it, the first growth from out of me, slow and yet fast, the beginning of birth. The wave, the energy and the noise are decreasing, the tide goes down as I float, as I roll in the foam, on the beach, light, alone, abandoned, alive.

Gertrude says, "Stay, my love." So again he gives her his long, gentle weight, he settles onto her breasts, onto her belly drenched with their sweat, and breathes strongly as waves upon her ear. He has stayed inside her, and my mother is moving her trap around him. She moves as I move on the beach, both bobbing on the same swell. The night is palpitating gently overhead. The stars belong to the three of us, the breeze belongs to the three of us. All awaits me now. I am going to grow, develop, come join the others, last out my time, fill up my space, matter.

My friend, the mechanic's dog, is howling to the moon, somewhere by the lake, out by the Seminary dam. Maurice says, "Do you hear that dog howling?" And my mother answers him, "I would have too, if I weren't so well brought up!" And they both laugh, shaking anew the wave on the beach where I am resting and where, soon, my friend the mechanic's dog will join me too. Imagine how well I shall greet him: finally I too know pain and pleasure, life.

For two days now, the awaited blood has not come. That's it: in the heart of your world, he is there. A little spot dancing in your vast breathing.

You rise and, in front of the sun-drenched window, you touch your belly. Blind, he can see by your skin, by your blood, he sees us. Like a diver who has touched the bottom with his head, dazzled, almost suffocated, shaken by a long shiver of triumph that greatly intimidates me, I come to you in the light, and remain silent. Now, he is the one who matters.